A Carteret Christmas

D'Artanya

Published by T'Ann Marie Presents, LLC

Four Years Before This Christmas

Ronika

Moving our things into a new house together was the easiest part. I just knew it was going to be a long ass, draining ass process. What I didn't know was that my kids were going to buck and buck hard. I couldn't lie, I needed to adjust to this new life myself. I was allowing them all the time they needed. Cease seemed to think everything would come together on its own, but he didn't know my children.

The house was a great single-family home; the problem was, we were three families. We did what families did, and we made the space work. Shatia and Rahleigh split the basement. Rahleigh wasn't home much anyway because she was always over at Keon's. Elayah and Qualik got the attic space. Thankfully, it wasn't one of those small crawlspaces because we wouldn't have had enough room, especially with Elayah's fast ass just having another baby. I was ready to put her and Lik assess out. If it wasn't for my grand babies, I would have.

Tynee shared a room with Cease's daughter, Elizabeth. They were four years apart. Tynee often complained about how messy she was. His son, Emmanuel, and Tyzee shared a room. Being only two years apart and far less dramatic, they got along great.

"You remember I told you that Melinda wanted to talk to me, right?" Cease hit the switch on the bedroom wall.

"Mmhm." Since moving in together, his ex-wife always needed to talk to him about something.

"Well," he got into bed, "she said that Emmanuel pushed another kid at a birthday party."

"Good for him."

Cease twisted his neck at me. "I wasn't singing his praises, Neek."

"Well, you should be." I rubbed my arms down with lotion before hitting the switch of the lamp on my nightstand.

"I'm concerned that the," he paused, "edginess of your children may rub off on my two."

"So, you're saying my kids are influencing your kids, negatively."

"Nobody said anything about anyone being negative." He began rubbing my feet. Cease thought that would distract me from the bullshit he was saying.

"But if you felt my children were having a positive impact, we wouldn't be having this conversation. Stop carrying me like I'm stupid. You're saying it without saying it."

"I'm just saying—"

"Cease, please get the fuck out of my face! Your punk ass kids could use some of my kids' edginess." I rolled my eyes at him and snatched my feet from his hands.

I wasn't even mad at him. I was pissed with myself. He said that slick shit about my children at the Christmas party at his family's house. I should've known better.

"Punks?" Cease stood from the bed. "They are ten and eight. What the fuck are they supposed to be doing?!"

"All I know is, they are too damn old to be crying and whining all the fucking time! They cry more than the newborn upstairs," I laughed.

"Do you mean Qua'layah or Qualik because if his grown ass could be attached to your breast, he would be."

I punched him in his mouth. "Let that be the last time you speak about my son like that. We'll work your ass in here."

I flipped the light switch and opened the door to leave, and Cease grabbed me and pushed me on the bed. "Let that be the last time you fucking hit me, Neek." He touched his lip to see if it was swollen, and I jumped on him, taking him down to the floor. I tried to bite that bitch's ear off. He finally got from under me and the second he did, Qualik was running into the room. He misread what he saw and landed a kick so hard to Cease's chest, he fell back down to the floor. Lik kicked his ass like he was kicking in a door.

"Lik, baby, relax." I stood in front of Cease. "It's fine. I was fucking him up, not the other way around." I held him off with my hands.

"Well, Tyzee came running up the steps, saying he called the police because Cease was screaming and hitting you."

"He must've been peeking through the door," I put my hands to my head, "Cease only pushed me on the bed. That's it. I fucked him up, Lik. Look at his face." I pointed to Cease's face.

"You said he ain't do shit, now you saying he pushed you. Ma, I will blow this nigga off the fucking earth!" Lik yelled, and his chest heaved up and down.

"Go the fuck upstairs!" I pointed him out of my room. "Elayah! Come get Lik."

That quick, the house turned into chaos. I was trying to calm Lik down because he thought he could beat anybody's ass, but I wasn't sure he could fuck with Cease. The man was a firefighter. He had strength that Lik couldn't fuck with. My son was smart. He knew that — which meant he was going to fight dirty, and it was uncalled for because I fucked Cease up on my own.

"Daddy!" Elizabeth was calling for her father. "The police are at the door."

"I'm coming, baby." Cease shook his head at me. I stood in front of Lik to keep them off of one another as Cease went down the steps to handle the police.

"Come on, Lik. Let's go. Y'all done woke my baby up." Elayah stood at the bottom of the attic steps, patting the baby on his back.

"Girl, he will go back to sleep. We got more serious shit going on. Keep his ass upstairs." I pointed the both of them and the baby up the steps.

By the time I grabbed my robe to cover my night shorts and tee, the police were putting Cease in the back of their car.

"Officer, what's going on?" I ran down the front steps to the officer still standing in front of the door while the squad car that held Cease pulled off. "Why is he being taken into custody?"

"We got a call from a very panicked little girl reporting a domestic dispute. When he came down the steps, the little one," he pointed to Tyzee, who was standing on the porch in his pajamas and slippers, "pointed him out to us."

"He mistook what he saw. This is all a misunderstanding. I don't want to press any charges."

"If that's the case, you should be able to go down to the precinct and explain that. But nothing can be done until he is processed."

"Thank you, officer."

"Very welcome, ma'am." He went to his car, and I stormed up the steps.

When I got the front door closed, I lit Tyzee a new one. "You so fucking nosey! Why would you do that, Tyzee? Calling the police is very serious. Now Cease has to go to jail. Do you understand what you just did?"

"He was hitting you!" Tyzee cried.

"No, he wasn't! I was hitting him!" My hands shook as I spoke. "This is why you need to stop creeping around here in everybody's business! Take your ass to bed!"

When I walked past Tynee, she rolled her eyes at me.

"Do it again and I'll knock them out your head!"

I was so pissed with him. Cease didn't have a career where getting arrested was no big deal. He put our entire livelihood on the line with that dumb ass phone call.

Three Years Before This Christmas

Shatia

"Woooo! Yeah, Sha! That's my girl!" Israel made sure to embarrass me as I left the karaoke stage.

Only drunk me was bold enough to do that, and it was hard enough without Israel adding to it.

"Stop, stupid!" I shoved him, laughing as I sat in my seat next to him.

"What?" he shrugged. "You did great up there." He pointed to the stage.

I rolled my eyes at him and took one of his nachos. We spent the day together in celebration of me being finally being able to do my own thing with this hair shit. I was exactly where I saw myself. The only thing I was missing was Israel. I had him, but I was ready for us to be together, together.

"Yeah, whatever, nigga. It's your turn."

The main thing stopping me from pursuing a relationship was Kina. She and I were no longer friends. Nothing crazy happened with us; we just fell off. Secretly, I think she had an issue with me and Israel's friendship. I didn't know what to do about that. I felt keeping our relationship strictly platonic was more than enough. One day, I just stopped calling, and so did she.

"Love," Israel belted out the words to Musiq Soulchild's song.

He stared at me while he sang and for the first time, I wasn't uncomfortable. I felt every note. Tonight was the night I would push my anxiety to the side and reveal my feelings.

When Israel parked in front of my house to drop me off, I did it. I made my move and kissed him deeply.

"I'm ready to be your girlfriend," I confessed.

Israel's face turned to worry. He bit his lip and shook his head. "We have the worst timing in the world."

"What's wrong? Why is now not a good time?"

"Shatia," he exhaled. "I took you out to celebrate you, but I also have something to tell you."

My heart broke before I knew what he would say. A million scenarios had gone through my head before I even made my move. I didn't need to know which one was about to play out, knowing nothing of what he was about to say would be what I wanted to hear.

"I joined the military. I leave in a week."

"You fucking bastard!" I punched him in his chest. "I fucking hate you! I don't ever want to talk to you again."

I rushed out of his car and into the house.

"What's wrong with you?" Lik asked.

"I fucking hate Israel!" I screamed, just as Israel was knocking at the door.

"That's him at the door?" Lik didn't hesitate to answer it. He swung the door open and punched Israel in his face. "Get the fuck off my porch, bitch."

"Lik, what are you doing? He didn't do anything!" I rushed back over to the door, before Lik had a chance to swing on him again.

"Well, what the fuck you come in the house crying and shit for?" Lik twisted his face. "Y'all be on some goofy ass shit, bruh." Lik turned the living room TV off and went upstairs.

"I'm sorry," I told Israel before slamming the door in his face.

"Mommy! Shatia crying!" Tynee yelled.

"Shut up, Tynee. You always telling something."

Ever since Tyzee got in trouble for running his mouth, it was like Tynee was using her voice for him.

I loved that Lik punched Israel though, because that's what I wanted to do. I went into my room and had a whole panic attack about him leaving. I couldn't stop crying. My heart felt like it was breaking in two. I couldn't breathe at the thought of Israel no longer being a part of my day to day.

Two Years Before This Christmas

Rahleigh

"I don't want to hear the shit, Rahleigh. You did this shit to yourself."

Keon was not swayed by any of my whining about being on house arrest. They might as well put me in jail. He wouldn't stop reminding me that he told me this would happen. I think he was secretly happy that I got caught stealing and now had a record.

"It's not fair that you get to go out and enjoy life while I'm stuck here. You should be in here with me."

"You must be out your fucking mind, Leigh." Keon twisted his neck at me. "I'm not sitting in the house like I'm on house arrest. I told you to stop doing that dumb shit. You wanted to go behind my back, so that's on you.

"Whatever. Go wherever the fuck you going. I'm tired of hearing that shit." I shoved him out the front door.

It'd only been a week, and I was over it. I had a year and half left on this damn box. I wasn't going to make it, especially since I couldn't smoke or drink. I did the next best thing I could think of.

I went into Ma Free's room and grabbed her pill bottle. I remembered Keon saying he had to go to the pharmacy, so I went ahead and grabbed the last pill in the bottle. She was sleep for the night, so she didn't need it.

As I got a glass of water to swallow the pill, I read the prescription. According to the bottle, she shouldn't have had no less than ten pills left.

"Rahleigh!" She called out to me.

I swear her ass was knocked out when I went into her room. I didn't know how she knew I grabbed her bottle, but I knew that was what she was calling me for.

"Yes?" I walked into her room.

"Where my pills at? Keon been to the pharmacy, yet?"

"You took them all. He's going in the morning." I slapped my hand on my thigh, letting her know she was out of options.

She glanced down at her bottle in my hand. "You took my shit, bitch. I had ten pills left."

My mouth dropped at her lie. "You a motherfucking lie. You had one pill left, and I took it because I needed it more." I rolled my eyes at her.

We used to get along so well but being at the house twenty-four seven, allowed me to see another side to her. I now realized it was addiction. It only took that week to see it.

"You better take your ass out there and get me some more pills. I don't care if you get them off the street. You better get them, or I'm telling Keon you in here taking my shit like Skittles."

"How the fuck am I supposed to do that?" I shook my ankle, showing my ankle bracelet.

"Not my fucking problem. Go get my shit, little girl."

If it wasn't for me being so scared of Keon finding out, I would've cursed her old, fat ass out. I didn't make it past the front gate before my shit started beeping. I let it beep as I ran down to the corner.

I handed a twenty to the first nigga I saw, and he gave me one perc before passing me a five-dollar bill back. I ran the pill in the house to Free. I tossed it on the bed and made her look for it because fuck her.

When Keon walked in that night, I met him at the door.

"We have to talk."

"What's wrong?" Keon gave me his full attention.

"Your mom."

"Is she ok?" He made movements towards the steps.

I grabbed his arm, and we walked over to the couch. I sat with one leg bent on the couch, my face resting on my arm that was using the back of the couch as an armrest. Keon let his hand fall onto my thigh.

"What's up?"

"I think your mom is struggling with the percs. According to the bottle, she should have ten left."

"Ok," Keon shrugged, taking his arm from my leg. "So, she took a few more than prescribed. She's in pain, Leigh."

"Keon, you're not in here with her. You don't hear the way she talks to me. She sent me outside to get her a fucking fix, my nigga."

"And you did it?!"

"I didn't want to do the shit, but you soft about your mother. I thought that's what you would want," I shrugged. "What was the alternative?" I stood from the couch.

"I don't fucking know, Leigh. I need to clear my head." Keon left the house.

When the door closed behind him, I couldn't get to the bathroom quick enough. I locked myself in. I leaned over the toilet seat, forcing myself to throw up. I was just going to have to do probation sober because addiction wasn't worth it for me.

One Year Before This Christmas

Tasaya

"Hello?" I answered Jae's call. It was 5:15 AM. He promised to call me before my day got started. I set my alarm for 5:13 to make sure I didn't miss the call. I tried to steal all the sleep I could these days, but Jae was always the exception.

"Good morning, baby." I cheesed into the FaceTime.

"Morning, love," Jae sighed. "I don't know how you get prettier every day."

"'Cause I'm being loved by you." We were staring into each other's eyes. You couldn't tell me he wasn't right in the room with me.

I felt him all around me at all times. At this point, he was a part of me.

"I can't wait to kiss you."

"You better make it good, too. I want tongue sucking, lip biting, and ass grab — the works!" I hollered into the phone.

"I was thinking a peck like one of them sexy ones where we push our lips out, and we can hear the smacking sound." He smushed his lips together.

"Boo, nigga. We don't want that."

"Well, you and your personalities gon' have to take what you can get."

Multiple knocks at the door let me know it was time for us to get off the phone.

"They're here. I have to go. Seen you soon?"

"In five hours and some change. I love you, Say."

"I love you, too, Donjae," I smiled, hanging up the phone.

He would never hang up first. He would just stare until I hung up. I hated hanging up first, but one of us had to.

"Tasaya, wake yo' ass up!" Ma Neek yelled from the other side of the door.

"I'm coming." I couldn't help but giggle at her excitement.

I opened the door and Elayah jumped into my arms. "I'm so happy for you!"

"Girl," Ma Neek scrunched her face up at Elayah. "Relax before Shatia has a fucking panic attack."

We joked about Shatia's panic attacks as if they weren't a serious thing. She hadn't had one since last year when Israel came home to visit with a wife and a baby. She was doing a lot better, and that was because of the weed, courtesy of my brother Yahsir, better known as Yah Yah. After Rowdy and Rolla decided to move to Maryland, Yah Yah wanted in on the action, well the bitches. Uncle Damon helped Jae and me get a house, and I let my brothers have Ma Pearl's house. It was a full-on bachelor pad. All they did was smoke weed and fuck bitches.

"Ha!" Shatia yelled. "I already got a blunt in me. I knew when I got up that I wouldn't be able to handle all the extraness of today." Shatia gave me a kiss on the cheek as she walked past me.

"Please, stop being so loud," Leigh whined. "I'm hungover." Rahleigh laid across my bed.

"I bet you are with all them shots you had. Keon would kill you if he saw the way you were rubbing all over that stripper last night," I told her.

"I was?" Leigh raised her head. "Fuck. Please don't tell Keon."

"You need to be worried about your probation officer," Ma Neek told her.

“Don’t tell that bitch either,” Leigh mumbled, refusing to lift her head from the pillow.

“Delete these pictures I have, you say?” Elayah shook her phone with a smirk.

“You got one, too?” Shatia laughed.

“One? I got a few!” Elayah unlocked her phone and showed Shatia the pictures.

“Yeah, aight. I’ll beat both of you the fuck up.” Rahleigh adjusted the pillow under her head and laid back down.

“And Keon gon’ fuck you up.”

“Gah, I can’t wait to see Keon in his suit,” I gushed.

“It’s your wedding day. What are you worried about him for?” Shatia sucked her teeth.

“She just mad that she ain’t gang,” Rahleigh mumbled.

“Alright, alright, shut up. We gotta get Tasaya ready.” Ma Neek couldn’t handle all the back and forth like she used to. She was an irritated grandma now. She never lost her patience with the kids, though. “Come on and start her makeup, child.” She pointed Elayah to the mirror.

There was nothing they could do to get me more ready to marry Jae. My dress was beautiful, but I’d walk down the aisle in nothing if he was on the other side. Since I met him, I’d been following his footsteps. I may have looked like the leader, but the goal was his. I was just helping him get to it. There’d never been a time where taking care of him wasn’t taking care of myself in return. He always paid back with interest.

“Mommy!” Savion was banging on the connected suite door.

Elayah hit her toe, trying to run and hide in the bathroom. She had just wrapped up on my makeup, and Shatia was getting ready to do my hair. We were running behind on the strict schedule we were on.

“Tynee, we told you to keep him occupied for a few hours,” Ma Neek complained as she opened the door, and my little baby ran to me with a bottle in his hand.

He was two, and I was trying to ween him off the bottle, but he wasn’t having any of it. He’d have a full-on tantrum. He loved to throw things and make shit fall off the wall. He never did it when Jae was home, and he never gave Jae as much trouble either. Still, Jae couldn’t get him to do anything that he didn’t want to do either. If Jae tried to make him eat his vegetables, he would cross his arms and stare away from us. The boy was a vicious combo of the both of us.

“He bit me!” Tynee yelled, shoving her wrist in her mother’s face.

“Savion,” I raised my eyebrows.

“Huh?”

“I told you that you had to be good for Auntie Nee.”

“She not let me go! I want see you.”

How was I supposed to be mad at that? He was so cute.

“Girl, you so soft,” Ma Neek huffed. “Savion, take your ass back in there with Nee.”

“Always telling!” Savion yelled at Tynee.

He wasn’t lying. Tynee and Tyzee switched roles. Zee was the sneaky one now. Tynee told on everything and everybody. She was quiet, and all she did was read books, but still, nothing got by her. If Zee was quiet, it was probably because he was doing something he wasn’t supposed to be doing.

Tynee followed Savion inside of the other room and shut the door.

“She is always telling though,” Rahleigh mumbled.

Elayah cracked the bathroom door and looked around.

“They’re gone,” I laughed.

Qua'layah and Quay were in the suite with them. Elayah was hiding from them because they were as clingy as Qualik was. At four and three, they hardly talked to any of us, unless Elayah wasn't around. When we were all they had, they wanted to be our best friend. They were as funny acting as their mother was.

"Shatia! Do you have to yank my head like that? Damn," I sucked my teeth.

"I told you that your bun was going to have to be tight in order for it to stay in place. Otherwise, when you get on that dancing floor, twerking like you do, the shit is going to fall apart. You turning your head every which way, sit still then, shit."

Shatia was in therapy. That may have been another reason we hadn't seen a panic attack. The focus in therapy right now was speaking her thoughts out loud. Keeping it in was increasing her anxiety because the thoughts would never leave. Now she had verbal vomit and just said anything at any time.

When my bun was finished, Ma Neek helped me into my dress while my sisters rushed to get themselves ready.

"Are you ready?"

"Been ready to become a Carteret. I've always wanted sisters and a mom. I already have hella brothers, so it's nothing to add more. I'm about to marry the man that was made for me. I'm so ready, Ma."

Ma Neek smiled and gave me a tight hug. "And I believe it." She made a small adjustment to my bun. "But I was asking if you're ready for marriage."

"Ma, I know you have strong opinions about marriage, but Jae and I are both ready. We want this. Are we prepared for everything coming our way? Probably not. Is anyone ever prepared for anything? We'll figure it out along the way."

"It's hard, Tasaya. Marriage is hard."

Ma Neek was excited when Jae proposed. The closer we got

to the wedding, the more her fears started to show themselves. She hadn't said it out loud, but I knew. She didn't want us to get married. It wasn't our age or that she didn't like me. Up until this very moment, she hadn't verbally said anything. I wanted to know where it was coming from, but it was rare for Ma Neek to get deep.

"Maybe for you, but I'm not you. Jae is not Tykee. We are not Damon and Vanessa. We're not my mother and father. I don't want to be a forever girlfriend. I deserve more than that. I want this. And I want it with Jae."

"I know y'all love each other—"

"But?" I twisted my neck at her. She didn't say anything. "It's starting to feel like you don't think we have what it takes to make it."

"Tasaya." She stepped away from me. "Now you know—"

"Then what is it, Ma? You wait until I'm about to walk down the aisle to toss all of this on me."

"People die, Tasaya. One day, your life is magic and fucking rainbows and the next day, the sky is falling and all the magic is gone. There's nothing you can do to stop it. You have to control what you can."

I looked at her in sad wonder. "Is that why you won't marry Cease?"

She stopped looking at me through the mirror. "Ok, let me get a look at you." She moved around to be in front of me.

"Ma," I grabbed her wrists, "you know if Cease dies tomorrow, it's going to feel the same whether you're married or not, right?"

"Yesss, sis!" Rahleigh came into the room with a tray of shots. "Jae definitely gon' cry when you walk down that aisle." She sat the tray on the dresser.

"Please, Jae, don't cry." I waved her off as the kids came out of the backroom with Elayah and Shatia.

A knock at the door came adding to the commotion in the room. Ma opened the door, and it was my daddy.

"How you doing, Trench?" Ma gave him a hug.

"I'm here to pick up a princess." He made his way through the door and when he saw me, he grabbed his mouth.

"Hi, daddy." I fanned my eyes because he was about to make me cry.

"Alright, let's get this show on the road." Ma waved everyone out of the room.

"Damn." He stepped back from me. "I really do make beautiful fucking kids, man." He shook his head, and I burst into laughter. "You are beautiful, princess."

"Thank you, daddy."

"I can't imagine not being a part of this day. Let's do this shit." We dapped before he wrapped his arm in mine.

We walked from the room, through the lobby and to the ceremony door, holding hands. It felt good having my daddy back, but I couldn't wait for him to pass me off to Jae, Big Daddy.

Ten Days Before Christmas

Shatia

It was Lik's birthday, and it was a surprise to us all that all he wanted was a birthday dinner. He even requested that all of his birthday gifts be stuff for his kids. Best believe that I was that auntie and was going to splurge on the kids anyway. My clientele had grown, and the money was flowing in so well, that I was close to what I needed for a down payment on a loan for my own hair shop.

I walked into the backyard of Mommy's house. I wanted to hit the blunt before I had to go in and be cordial. I knew for a fact that at least one person was back there smoking.

Not to my surprise, Say's brothers, my brothers, and Israel and his brother, Jeru, were all out back already. I didn't even have to smoke what I had rolled and stuffed in my bra because I was added to the three separate rotations happening. I stood closest to Lik, shivering, because it was cold as shit. I didn't get but three hits before Ma showed herself.

"If y'all don't get y'all pothead asses in here, right now!" Ma yelled at all of us to go inside. "God see y'all trifling asses," she pointed.

We all hollered, and Ma couldn't help but to laugh at herself, too. I watched Israel tell Jeru to go ahead and he'd catch up to him. He was waiting for me.

"You look good," he told me.

"You look nice yourself. So, what's up? How's it feel to be home for good?"

Israel got an honorable discharge for an injury to his penis. He'd been living in California and only coming to Maryland to visit, but he'd finally convinced his daughter's mother to move to Maryland.

"Still getting used to it," he shrugged. "Just waiting on the part where things feel like they used to."

"What you mean?" I asked him, as we walked inside.

"When will things with us get back to normal?"

"Bring y'all asses in here. It's bad enough Shatia was late. We hungry as hell."

"We'll talk soon. I promise," I told him as we walked towards the house.

Israel called me twice since he'd been home. I didn't answer either call. I did send him a text, letting him know I was busy with clients. It was the truth, but I was avoiding him, too. When he came home all the other times, it was for a visit—two weeks at the most. It was easy to play on our chemistry when I knew he was leaving again. I was scared he wanted to talk about us being more, and I didn't want to talk about that.

"Uh oh, my man said he want that old thing back!" Lik yelled out, making everyone laugh except me.

I was embarrassed. I felt naked, like everyone could see through me. This is why I kept them out of my business because everything was a joke to them. This was my real life.

"You got an issue, nigga?" Jeru turned to Say's brother, Yah, and the room went silent.

"Jeru, sit yo' ass down and shut yo' ass up." Ms. Letty, their mom, tried to calm him down.

That was no use because Jeru had a few missing crayons. Anything could set him off and once he was, he was off. He usually made for good entertainment, but he wasn't that familiar with Yah yet, so I wasn't sure if he knew what he was getting himself into. Truthfully, I don't think he cared.

"With all due respect," Yah stood up. "It's too late for that." Yah swung, and Jeru stumbled back.

Everyone rushed in to break it up before it got any worse. The house was in full chaos as Mommy announced the party was over and everyone had to get the fuck out. I was fine with that because with everyone trying to get their hair braided before the holiday, I was tired. I cleared my schedule for the following day and had no plans of getting out of the bed until the sun came up and set again. I made sure to grab myself a plate before I left.

The one thing my therapist did help me with was moving out of Ma's. I liked Cease; he was good for Ma, but him moving in changed the dynamics of our house. I don't know, it could've been the fact that Leigh and Donjae weren't there. The twins spent a lot of time at Uncle Damon's after that whole incident with Cease going to jail. Home just stopped feeling like home for me one day. My therapist helped me get the courage to go on my own. She suggested that with the way I loved my privacy, it would be better for me. She was right.

Once I was home, I devoured my plate and jumped in the shower. When I stepped out of the bathroom, Yah was on my couch.

"I know you didn't drive over here drunk like that."

He was only in his boxers, and his eyes were barely open. They were always barely open, but I was certain the amount of weed and alcohol he consumed was a part of it. The scar in the center of his chest from where he got shot always turned me on.

"Rowdy dropped me off before he headed back home.

"You told him you were coming here?" I panicked.

Nobody knew we were fucking, and I wanted to keep it that way. All of Say's brothers were fine, but Yah Yah was closer to me in age. He had a tapered fade with a cruddy top, a perfectly trimmed circle beard, and he gave me my first high and my first orgasm.

"Yeah. Rowdy barely talks. We good." Yah began drying my body off with the towel.

"Barely talks? He tells you everything." I sucked my teeth.

"Yeah, me. That's my brother."

"I don't care. I told you I didn't want anyone to know. I don't want my family in my business."

"You worry too much about what other people think."

"And you don't worry enough." I cupped his chin. "I like my private moments private, Yah. And what was with the shit you pulled at my mother's? You can't just be fighting like that. The kids were there. They could've gotten hurt.

"You need to give that speech to that nigga, Jeru. I probably was looking at Israel a lil' crazy, but that was none of his fucking business, forreal."

"And why were you looking at him like that? That's his brother. I would've stepped about mine, and I know you would've stepped behind yours."

"Because I love you. Everybody keep joking about what you and that nigga Israel got going on. A nigga don't wanna hear that shit. I wish that nigga go back to wherever the fuck he was."

I kept quiet. Yah and I were sneaky links, and that was it. I mean, he had a key to my place and stayed over more nights than not, but we weren't together. For him to say he loved me like it was nothing, made me uncomfortable. I loved him too, but I didn't want everything to change by putting a title on our link. I just wanted to link.

"I guess I fucked up. What's my punishment?"

My favorite thing about Yahsir was that he liked to be dominated. I didn't know I was into dominating a man until the first time we fucked. He coached me through telling him what I wanted and how I wanted it until I was ordering him to shove his face in my coochie. Yah showed me my power. He sounded so good moaning while he ate me like I was his favorite food.

That was why I didn't want to talk to Israel. I was in love with another man.

Nine Days Before Christmas

Rahleigh

"What's wrong, Rocky?" Keon asked.

We were driving back home after dropping Jae and Say to the airport. I wanted to leave with them. Every Christmas, to celebrate their anniversary, they went on a trip. Gah, how I wanted that to be my life.

"Nothing," I lied, turning the music up in the car.

If I was honest about what was bothering me, it would only turn into an argument. Keon was really sensitive about his mother. He was as bad as my brothers. You couldn't say shit to any of them about their mothers, even if it was the truth. Anything that wasn't praising her, sounded like disrespect to them.

"Rahleigh, you clearly have a fucking attitude. What the fuck is the problem now?" Keon talked with one hand as he was driving.

He was frustrated. I was frustrated, and all we did lately was argue. The worst part was no make-up sex. I gained so much weight, sitting in the house on that house arrest bullshit that I didn't feel attractive anymore. I knew I was fine as fuck; I just couldn't see that when I looked in the mirror. This baby I was hiding was fucking with my hormones. That was the real reason we weren't having sex. I never intended to hide my pregnancy for this long, but I was too far now to announce it. They'd know I was pregnant when I went into labor. Then, they wouldn't be able to be mad at me.

I didn't say anything after I got the positive pregnancy test because I wanted to see a doctor first. Sometimes, those tests were wrong. I didn't want to have Keon riled up for nothing. After getting blood work done for a confirmation, I still didn't say anything because I was weighing my options. If Keon knew I was pregnant, he wouldn't be okay with an abortion, so I would have to do that in secret. Once the deadline passed to go through with that, Keon was always working. I got pissed that he was never home enough to notice that I was carrying our baby. So, hiding the baby became something I did out of spite. It got to a point where I felt like I should tell him, but then I kept thinking about how angry he was going to be, so I figured it was best to say nothing.

My days were spent taking care of Keon's mother. On top of the addiction she formed, her back was getting worse, and she was confined to the bed most of the time. She was always in pain. He was always gone, and I was always taking care of her. My life revolved around his mother so much, that when my mother was sick with the flu, I couldn't even help Cease take care of her.

This is not how I pictured life with Keon. I saw a big ass house, a fenced in yard with a four-car garage. Instead, we were in a two-bedroom apartment in an apartment building with parking spaces we had to fight over every time we came home. I hated this shit and if I was being honest, I was starting to hate him, too.

"Keon, go the fuck head," I said, barely above a whisper. My eyes were closed, and my head was resting against the headrest of the seat. "I'm not for this shit tonight. I just want to go to sleep so I can take care of your mother first thing in the morning." I knew I shouldn't have said it, but I didn't give a fuck.

"Again, with this shit," Keon shook his head, "You did this to yourself! You went and caught not one, not two, but three theft charges! I told your dumb ass to stop boosting from them rich people's stores and you said you stopped, but you lied!"

"And I did my house arrest! It's over with but somehow, I'm still locked down, taking care of your mother! That was not part of my punishment."

"Taking care of my mother is punishment? That's fucked up.

If it was your mother, I wouldn't hesitate to __"

"Because my mother has been a mother to you since the day I met you! She has been kind as fuck to you—giving, loving, everything your mother couldn't be for you.

"I hit the pavement every fucking day to take care of her fucking ungrateful ass daughter. You don't have to ask your mother or brothers for shit! I do it. All I ask is that you help me with my fucking mother."

"She's your mother and your responsibility! You should hear how your mother talks to me when you aren't around."

"Bet. So, this is what we're going to do. I'm going to get the money for my mother to have the surgery she needs. You are going to get a job and start paying your way around this motherfucker."

"Keon! You know nobody will hire me!"

"McDonald's will."

"You bugging. I'm not doing that shit."

"That's the problem! You don't want to do shit! You not tryna get a job. You not tryna help with my mother. It sounds like you want free time to run the streets while I'm busting my ass at work. That shit dead. You got me fucked up!"

When Keon got to cursing and yelling at me, he was serious. I didn't give a fuck because I was serious too. I was too young to be spending my time taking care of some rude ass bitch. I was too cute to be doing that fast food bullshit. I would find something else. If I had to work to get out of the house, then so be it.

The rest of the ride home was silent. I stared out of the window, watching the snow that started falling. Keon nodded his head to the music he was playing. I loved him, but if this was what being with Keon was going to look like from day to day, I wanted out. The problem was, I didn't want to be a single mother. I watched my mom do that shit, and it wasn't going to be me.

∞∞∞

The next morning, I woke up to the sound of church music and the smell of bacon. I glanced at the clock, and it said 10:00 AM. I jumped up because Free needed her meds at 9:00 AM. When I found Elayah sitting on my couch with a plate on my coffee table, I didn't know what to think.

"Good morning, Leigh." Elayah took a sip of her orange juice.

"What you doing here?" I tightened my robe.

I grabbed Free's pill container from the shelf in front of the TV and saw the pills for that morning were gone.

"Keon asked me to help with his mother. He said you had some job applications to do or something."

I was going to curse him out again for telling my business. I didn't want anyone to know I was looking for a job because everyone would keep asking if I got it. It would be embarrassing to keep saying I didn't. And he wasn't slick. I knew he had Elayah here as a babysitter to watch his mother and me.

If you wanted Elayah to keep a secret, you had to verbally tell her to shut the fuck up about it. And even then, sometimes she'd hit you with, 'I'm not comfortable keeping that secret.' So, there was a fifty/fifty shot in the dark that she was telling on your ass.

Since he was petty enough to have Elayah at the house, I was going to be pettier by leaving. I'd fill my applications out at the library. I took a shower, tossed on something warm, and let Elayah know I'd be back.

"Hey, if Keon asks, I'm—"

"Un unh, you know I do not get in the middle of relationship shit. You tell him where you're going, so he don't even have to ask me."

"Whatever," I mumbled, leaving the apartment.

Since having a second child, Elayah thought everyone was her child. She dealt with us like we were situations that needed to be handled.

I wanted a family with Keon before all of this shit happened. I wanted a bunch of kids like mommy had, and I wanted them to be super close like me and my siblings. I didn't want any of that anymore. I wanted to travel the world on a rich man's dime. I would've loved for Keon to be that rich man, but if it wasn't, then so be it.

Ronika

Something about the smell of coffee in the morning made me feel grateful to be alive, no matter what the day was going to bring.

I took my cup of coffee and headed to the front porch. Cease thought because it was winter, I would retreat to staying in the bed with him, but that was dead. This was my only opportunity for alone time. I had Lik connect my space heater through the window so that I could have some warmth. Cease warned me over and over that it was a fire hazard and with my past, I should've been terrified, but it was an hour a day, and we'd be fine. He ended up hiring an electrician to add an outlet to our porch.

It was a rainy morning. The sun was nowhere to be found, and the traffic on our street was light. This was what my peace was made of. I sat my coffee on my little table and opened the book Tynee and I were reading together. She was anxious to get her hands on the urban books that Shatia read. Cease told her she had to wait until she was at least fifteen. She was only eleven now. We were going to sneak and read because I was over this baby shit.

My front door came flying open and it was Lik, face screwed up and moving like he was about to go fuck something up.

"Come on, Qua'layah." Lik leaned against the screen door to hold it open. He had Quay bundled up tight in his arms.

"Boy, what the fuck is wrong with you?"

"I'm fitna knock your boyfriend the fuck out. Tell that nigga stop fucking talking to me!" He yelled as he grabbed Qua'Layah's hand to help her down the steps. He got them both in the car and pulled off.

He was probably on his way to Shatia's. They'd grown closer since Lik's daughter was born. Shatia loved being an auntie and helped Lik and Elayah out a lot. Whenever he got mad, he ran over there.

Cease had come up with a lot of rules. Well, we went over them together. He said we needed some structure, and I had to agree with him. Both of his children were well behaved, and I wanted a little of that to rub off on mine. Although, with Cease's arrest, Melinda was able to go back to court and now the arrangement was for them to share the kids fifty/fifty. Truthfully, I enjoyed not having them around because their goody two shoes asses made me feel like I had to be perfect, or they'd go running to their mother.

I thought we'd discussed structure for the twins, but Cease's focus seemed to be on Lik. Even the ones who didn't live with me were on Cease's ass. They felt like he was picking on Qualik, and they weren't with it. I had to beg Donjae to let Cease come to the wedding. Rahleigh wouldn't talk to him at all, and Shatia was short with him.

I was catching some of their wrath for him because they felt like I was just letting my man do whatever he wanted. It wasn't true. Cease and I were in constant arguments about the way he handled Lik. We had our arguments behind the doors of our bedroom, or in the car. One of Cease's rules was that we wouldn't argue in front of the kids, and that we'd keep them out of our relationship business. He felt they were grown because I kept them in my business like they were my peers, instead of my children.

The way I saw it, they were human. They weren't blind to what I had going on, so I kept them in the know. With the secret I held for so many years, I had to be upfront with them about shit. Cease didn't understand that. He thought he was going to keep me in line the way he kept his baby mother in line, but I wasn't her. I went along with the shit I agreed with and fought him tooth and nail on the rest.

Cease came rushing out the front door not too long after. “You need—”

“Nope.” I held my hand up. “I got ten more minutes before Savion gets up. Leave me alone.”

He stood there, looking stupid before he decided to get the fuck out of my face. I took all of my ten minutes before going inside. I had perfect timing because Savion was using his hands and feet to get down the steps backwards. He held his bottle with his teeth.

“It makes no fucking sense that he still has a bottle,” Cease scoffed.

“Hey GG baby, good morning.” I scooped him up when he made it to the bottom step, completely ignoring Cease.

Savion wrapped his arms around me and squeezed tightly. He gave the cutest hugs. “Bacon, please.” He talked well, but all the Carterets did. Probably because of all the talking going on around them.

Day to day, we never knew what he would eat or refuse, but one thing was for sure — he always wanted bacon.

“Let’s get that baby some bacon.” I tickled his stomach as I carried him into the kitchen.

“I’m a big boy, GG.”

“Well, big boys don’t use bottles.” We all wanted Savion off the bottle, but everything we tried hadn’t worked. He’d give it up eventually. What wasn’t helping was Cease reminding us every chance he got. I tried to take the bottle from Savion’s hands, but he pulled away and threw it to the floor.

I put him down and popped his thigh. “Go pick that shit up, Savion.” He didn’t even flinch from the pop, but he picked his bottle up like I told him.

Savion could be a handful if you let him. Tasaya was against beating him, but we were clear that if I was watching him, I was going to pop his ass.

"Get in your seat." I pointed to his booster seat at the table.

I was counting down the days until January second. At least Thanksgiving and the birthdays were out of the way. When Jae and Say came back from their anniversary vacation, I was taking Savion to the airport to meet them. He didn't give me as much trouble as he gave them, but I needed sleep. I still had to get through Christmas and then New Year's. Nothing was going to stop me from getting all my sleep come January second.

I let Savion play for a little while after breakfast and around noon, he was down for his nap. If he didn't get a nap, he would be a headache for the rest of the day. I knew that headache was unavoidable when I came back down the steps, and Cease muted the TV.

"We need to talk about Qualik." Cease ran his hand down the back of his head.

I ignored him and walked into the kitchen. I grabbed some Motrin from the cabinet and popped two with a bottled water.

"Neek, did you hear me?" Cease followed me into the kitchen.

"Talk, Cease," I exhaled, showing my frustration.

"Really, Neek?"

"What? You want to talk, then talk. You don't want to have a conversation. You want to dictate, and it's not happening so waste your breath and talk."

"Why am I wasting my breath?"

"Because you've said the shit already, and I said what I said. Qualik is my child. He's going to stay home as long as he needs to."

"Him being here is not the problem; he needs to pay his own way. He's got a girlfriend, two kids—"

"Two kids he takes damn good care of. That's where his money goes. I pay his way when I pay mine."

I made $3600 a month from renting out my house. Damon paid the yearly fees so the money I made, I kept. Cease insisted that I not pay any bills, but I paid the insurance on my car, the gas and electric bill, the water, and I paid for the cable. My account was a nice nest should I need to separate from his ass.

"God forbid, you die tomorrow, what is he going to do?"

"Excuse me? Are you saying that if something happens to me, you're putting my son out?"

"I'm saying he needs to take care of himself and his family. There's not a single bill that comes in his name. Between you and Elayah, he doesn't have to cook, wash clothes, or clean up after himself because y'all do it all for him."

"I do the same exact shit for your children, and you, nigga. You want to talk about someone not cleaning up after themselves? How 'bout your two don't even like to take showers? I don't say shit when they sit their funky asses on my sofa." Cease stood there with his mouth hung open. "Don't feel good, do it, nigga? You take care of yours and I'll take care of mine. You don't discipline mine, and I won't discipline yours. That's how we'll do this shit from here on out. Don't say shit else out the way to my son."

I walked away for him. If he didn't stop playing with me, I was going to have Nee and Zee beat his kids' asses and give him some real shit to complain about. Elizabeth had Nee by four years, but I knew she could take her. Cease wanted to keep taking bout Qualik while I was worried about Rahleigh. She was hiding something and whatever it was, was hurting her. I was trying to give her the space to figure it out, but she'd had better figure it out soon.

Qualik

Qua'Layah made me love being a father, but Quay made me love being a man. My daughter made me gentler, quieter. I held my hand closer to my chest until it was time to lay the cards down. Quay made me mature. He brought back memories I lost of my father. Every day was like déjà vu with him.

"I'm sick of that nigga, Sha." I was pacing her living room as we shared a blunt.

Cease always had something to say to me. If it wasn't about me personally, it was about Elayah having an attitude or my kids being too loud, as if Savion wasn't a No Limit soldier. He never opened his mouth to say shit to Donjae, though. That nigga had a personal problem with me. I hated to be one of them niggas but if you asked me, he was jealous. I was my mommy's favorite, and he thought that shit was going to change once they moved in together. He was a hating ass nigga.

"I know, Lik. But it's his house, too. If you don't like it, you know what you have to do," Shatia shrugged.

"Beat that nigga's ass. Mommy gon' be mad as fuck with me, though." Shatia and I laughed.

"No nigga, you gotta move out. You see what I did. I saw that shit getting worse. My scary ass is living alone and loving it."

"I can't afford that shit, Sha."

"Then maybe it's time to consider letting Elayah work full time." She bit her lip.

"Then we would need full time daycare. I don't want her

working as is."

Elayah was a caregiver for the elderly. She loved it, but I hated it for her. She was taking care of someone's parents when her primary responsibility was our children and me. I wanted to take care of the bills while she took care of home. Elayah was determined to do both. I didn't like it, but she wasn't letting up, so I agreed to some part-time shit. I worked the beginning of the week while she worked the end. One of us was always home with our children because I didn't want to rely on Mommy too heavy. It would only be more shit for Cease to complain about.

"Realistically, you don't make the kind of money to have a stay-at-home woman. So, either kick it up a notch, or let her work full-time. She wants to work, Lik. Y'all can grind together. You'll figure out the rest as you go. Everyone does."

"No, everyone doesn't. That's why we got homeless people, niggas doing life sentences, and addicts," I counted with my fingers. "They couldn't figure that shit out."

"I feel you, but Cease gon' make you fuck him up. He called the cops on his ex-wife; I know he'll call them on your ass."

"I can't believe mommy is with this bitch ass nigga," I exhaled. "I'll be back in like an hour.

"An hour, Lik!" she called out to me as I shut her door.

Shatia and I had gotten closer since fucking them people's store up. She never had an issue with watching my two, even if it was last minute. Sometimes, I stopped by just so we could blow together. If she knew something was wrong and I wouldn't talk to her; she went around me to Elayah to make sure I was good. She kept my temper in check but held me down when she knew I was right.

Before she moved out, she cursed Cease out so bad, mommy made dinner two weeks straight because she felt so bad. Cease ain't even do shit to her. He called me a bum, or something close to it, and she went off on him. I could tell her anything.

I wasn't going to tell her this, though. In her speaking up for herself, she was going to tell me not to do it, and I didn't need a bunch of negativity in my ear. Keon got out the streets when Jae did, but during the holiday season, he jumped back in. My sister was expensive. Last year, he tried to put me on, and I turned him down. I'd just started the job I had now, and I was giving it a real go. The shit was cool, but the money wasn't coming fast enough. I needed money quick, so I could get my name on a lease. I'd figure out the rest later.

I pulled up on Keon at the garage he worked in. He did everything from detailing, painting, and small shit like brakes. He had made a good name for himself around the city. His company was called Get Keyed. Everyone in the streets called him Key now.

I opened my car door and let my umbrella pop open, so I wouldn't get wet at all. Keon was shielded from the rain by the garage.

"Yo, I need in on ya Christmas hits."

"Damn, nigga. What's up? How you? Shit." Keon twisted his neck.

"What? You on ya period, nigga? Hi, damn." I extended my hand for dap.

"I think your sister is on hers, and she getting on my fucking nerves." He took a pull from his cigarette.

"That's y'all business. But what's up with this money?"

I learned from Elayah to not involve myself in my siblings' business. If Keon got to venting, or if Tasaya told Elayah some shit about Donjae, I'd be ready to fuck shit up. I'd end up making shit worse than it needed to be. Then, they'd both be mad at me.

"No, yo," Keon said, moving around to check on his workers.

"What you mean, no? You ain't even give that shit no thought, for real." I followed behind him.

"Don't need to," he plucked his cigarette, "I don't steal no more. Ya sister made that shit hot. I'm in on something else, and I don't need no help."

"Good 'cause I'm not tryna share. All I need you to do is tell me where to go. Put me on how to move. That's it."

"No, nigga. You don't listen, and you don't like to do your dirt by yourself. You gon' have Rehaan, and whoever else you can find, going along for the ride. No, nigga."

"Rehaan my man. When I eat, he eat." Rehaan was not going to be with the shit. He'd been keeping his hands squeaky clean since coming home. Nigga was always taking the righteous path. He stayed with Salem since being released. Nigga was getting his shit together. I was happy for him, but I was tryna get my hands in the mud.

"See," Keon shook his head. "I'm not doing it, yo."

"That's fucked up," I pointed my fingers in his face, "you was my last resort, Key!" I yelled out as I walked backwards to the car. He shook his head and went back to the job.

I knew the real reason Keon told me no. He didn't want no smoke with Jae. Donjae was all the way legit, and I knew he would say no to me doing anything illegal, but this nine to five shit wasn't bringing in the money fast enough. He made out with it because Uncle Damon put him on with general contracting. To be fair, he tried to get me in on some house shit too, but I couldn't do that school shit. Now, it was looking like an L.

Now, I had to reach out to Jeru. He was always offering to put me down with some work but because of Israel and Shatia's weird relationship, I steered clear of him. I wasn't sure what he was into exactly but whatever it was, he made good money. The only thing I wasn't fucking with was the drugs. I promised mommy and Elayah I wouldn't touch it no more.

"Lik, I'm in the middle of some pussy this bitch made me wait for. What's up?" Jeru answered his phone.

I could hear the girl moaning in the background and looked

at my phone in disgust. This was already looking like a bad idea but when it came to my family, no idea was a bad idea if I could put them in a better position.

"I wanted to holla at you about some work."

"I got some big shit coming up. Be ready when I call."

"I'm ready, yo."

"Bet." Jeru ended the call.

I didn't even know what the fuck I was supposed to be ready for.

Eight Days Before Christmas

Donjae

I told Tasaya she could go anywhere in the world for our first anniversary, and she chose Bali. It was the rainy season, but I told her I would make her dreams come true, and that was what she wanted. It was the most beautiful place I'd ever seen. Still, it wasn't as beautiful as her.

Say was snuggled up under my arm with damn near all of her body on mine. She started doing that when I still had a toe in the streets. She wanted to know if I was getting out of the bed.

Her ass was poking through the blanket. It'd gotten fatter since she had Savion. Titties were bigger, too. The biggest change was that she sported a permanent glow. She kept telling me she was in her soft era. She was soft now. Cried at the drop of a dime, forgave all of her brothers and Trench. She had even let Missy back in, but I blocked that bitch every chance I could. Tasaya may have forgiven her, but I hadn't.

She fell back from teaching me the ways of the streets and let me do my own thing once she felt I'd learned enough. Rowdy and Rolla both showed me some shit that Tasaya couldn't.

Mama would tell me that when I had my own kid, I would understand some of her decisions. If anything, a lot of the shit the adults around me did, made even less sense to me now. I wanted to protect Savion and my niece and nephew above anything else. So, when Tasaya came to me with her worries about me in the streets, I respected it. Now, we were raising our little family the right way.

My son was the best parts of me and Say. They joked about how wild he was, but he had more personality and feelings than he knew what to do with. He'd grow into that shit and use it to excel. He looked exactly like me, and Say was hating hard. He was a full-on mama's boy though, so it was a fair exchange. I had my own family with the most beautiful woman in the world. This was a real nigga's dream.

I only wished that I would've kept my word and got out the game, but that shit wasn't easy — especially when Jeru came to me, wanting an in. It wasn't like I introduced him to the game or nothing. The nigga who put him on wasn't working out for whatever reason. I figured I could keep a toe in if I was the plug. If Tasaya knew, she'd feel like I was stepping further into the game, but I was hands off, other than the pick-ups and the drops.

I told Jeru that the only condition was that he not tell anyone that we had business dealings. Even Santi thought I was getting work for myself. Literally, nobody knew but me and Jeru. I tried to talk Say Say into a five-day trip by telling her that we couldn't be away from Savion that long, but she wasn't going for it. She refused anything less than seven days. Day six was my pickup with Santi, and I would be out of the country. I wasn't going to have a choice but to send Jeru.

"Hey, daddy." Tasaya opened her eyes.

"'Bout time you woke up." I kissed her lips.

"I don't know how you expect me to stay up for long when every hour, on the hour, you got your dick in me."

I made sure she got to see the sites. She did a lot of shopping. We tried a new restaurant every night. I made sure she was enjoying the trip fully. But we only had a few days left, and I was using them to give her all the dick I could give her while I could give it to her.

Work kept me gone most of the day. At first, Say would complain but now, all she asked was that I was home before Savion went to bed and that I answered all of her phone calls. I went the extra mile and called her, so she didn't have to call. I wouldn't go too long without talking to her.

Her brothers being here helped, especially Yah Yah. He was the male version of Rahleigh, always doing the most and ready to go.

"I'm tryna put something else in you." I pulled her naked body on top of mine.

"Oh yeah?" She slid me into her. "Like that?" she smirked.

"Like another baby." I grabbed her hips and stroked into her.

"You serious?" She put her hand on my stomach to stop my strokes.

"Didn't you ask for another baby?"

"I did, but I didn't think you were ready. You said—"

"Fuck what I said. I want everything you want." I started stroking into her, controlling her hips to move how I wanted them to.

The only time Tasaya glared at me was when she was riding. She always rode me like I pissed her off. Say made slow and deliberate bounces while never breaking eye contact. The breaths she took were released in huffs and puffs as if they were weighted. I was so connected to her; I could feel that shit in my stomach.

When my dick hit her cervix, she winced into a moan that sounded like she wanted more. The sound made my dick jump inside of her. That always made her lose it. Her breaths were shorter, her moans louder and higher. Her walls tightened around my dick and made my legs shake. I wrapped my hand around her neck. She took one of her breasts into her mouth and let spit fall down her chest as she came on my dick. She fell limp against my chest. In the lowest voice, she begged me to keep fucking her. I didn't last much longer because everything about my wife drove me crazy. I held her ass cheeks open while I pumped my nut into her.

Shatia

One of my clients reached out, letting me know that she'd contracted the flu. While she was still willing to get her hair done, I wasn't willing to risk my health for a check. I cancelled her appointment and refunded her deposit, and that was something I never did. The appointment was free for all of twenty minutes when Israel booked an appointment. I was annoyed and flattered at the same time. I didn't like that he was finding other ways to be in my space, but I also liked that he was finding other ways to be up under me. Something about fighting for love did it for me.

All the anxiety flowing through my body had me jittery and overthinking every conversation that led to the moment of him knocking on my door. I gave myself a pep talk to calm down before opening the door. When I opened it, everything went away. No worries, no fears, no obsessive thoughts that I couldn't control.

"Hi." He walked into my apartment without waiting for an invite.

"Hey." I shut the door behind him.

"So, what's up? What's with the weird shit?" He sat on the love seat with his arms stretched across his knees as one hand held tightly to his wrist, like it would fall if he let it go. "I call, you don't answer. You turned the read messages off, so I wouldn't know you were ignoring me. Did I do something to you?"

"No. No. You didn't do anything."

Israel and I remained best friends, no matter what was going on. He was the first person I told about anything I had going on or any of my family tea. So, it was hard not to tell him about what

I had going on with Yah Yah when everything felt comfortable. Familiar. Israel felt like home when home no longer felt like home. He hadn't changed any. If I told him about Yah, it would change everything. He wouldn't look at me the same. That was scary.

"Then what's wrong?"

"I don't know." I held my hands out in front of me, as if I was holding a baby. "I was excited for you to get home as I always am. When I saw you, I just," I exhaled. "You're home for good, Israel. I don't know what you think this means for us or what I want it to mean for us. It's just a lot."

"I didn't ask for anything to change. I respected the decision you made; it feels like you don't even want that anymore. What, you got a nigga or something?"

"No," I said quickly.

It wasn't a lie, though. Yah Yah and I were not boyfriend and girlfriend. We were just having fun. Well, I thought we were until he confessed that he loved me the other night. I hadn't dealt with my feelings from that yet, and here Israel was, trying to get me to deal with this heavy shit. I was supposed to work through one thing at a time, according to my therapist, and that was why I said the bitch wasn't worth a damn because real life didn't work like that. I had multiple things going on at once. How was I supposed to focus on one thing at a time?

"Shatia, don't lie to me, yo." Israel bent his head to his hands.

"I'm not. I'm not seeing anyone."

"So, this is just how things are going to be with us for good? We just cool? You gon' keep ignoring me, and I'm going to keep calling for how long, Sha?"

That shit cut me. It sounded like he was saying he was going to quit on me eventually. I didn't know what I wanted, but I knew I didn't want that. He was my best friend.

"I'm sorry. I'll do better. You call, I answer. You text, I text back immediately like always." I threw up the peace sign. That was our sign to one another that it was the two of us against everything.

"Good. I need to go Christmas shopping, and I booked you for the next seven hours. I want my money's worth."

"You gon' pay me for my time, too." I put my hat, gloves, and scarf on. "Why would you book the most expensive thing on my service list?" I zipped my coat up and rolled my eyes at him.

"Because you kept playing with me. I'm gon' give you your money. Don't expect no Christmas gift, though."

I slapped his arm before locking my apartment door behind us.

In the car, I compared Yah Yah and Israel. Israel was the dominant one in our relationship. He led, I followed. I felt safe with him, like zero to no anxiety when I was with him. I liked that part, but I didn't like that he had more control over us than I did. With Yah, I had all the control. He was affectionate and showered me with words of affirmation. He was the perfect blend of a sweet hood nigga, and I was weak for how powerful he made me feel. I didn't like that outside of the bedroom, he was nonchalant. It was like he didn't care anything for me unless I was manhandling him.

My heart was telling me to choose Israel. I knew he'd never hurt me intentionally. We were best friends. I was his daughter's godmother, and his family was basically a part of my family. It'd be easy to switch to a romantic relationship. But my pussy was telling me that Yah Yah was the one. He helped me tap into my power, and a strong man allowing me to be dominant was tingling my spine at just the thought. Plus, Yah was basically family, too. That was what made things complicated between us, if we were to get serious. Technically, he was my brother-in-law. I couldn't imagine being without either of them.

Damon

I was getting all four kids today. They were staying with me through the weekend. Vanessa was supposed to be here any minute now. Most times, I picked the girls up and dropped them back off but sometimes, it worked better for her to bring them to me. I did my best to not bring her any static. I always gave her a time that was an hour before Tynee and Tyzee would arrive. Tyzee hadn't softened up to her since their big fallout. Every time he saw her, she was every name he could think of. Little nigga didn't care about punishment or me whipping his ass; he took it on the chin to be able to disrespect her. Vanessa threatened to keep Nisha and Risha away if he didn't stop, so I came up with something that made sense.

"Hey daddy," the girls said at the same time. All the kids had keys, so they could come and go as they needed. Nee and Risha were always forgetting something, and I couldn't always get away from work.

"Hey, babies." I hugged them both at the same time. "I missed y'all."

"We missed you, too, Daddy."

"Go put y'all stuff down so I can talk to your father," Vanessa told them.

My frustration showed with a vocal exhale. I didn't need to know what she wanted to know she was about to get on my nerves. There was nothing we needed to talk about ever.

When the seasons changed, I took all four of them shopping for new clothes. If I needed to get them to the doctor or school, the kids were old enough to communicate with me directly. So, whatever she wanted to talk about was some shit we didn't need to talk about.

"So, I told you that I was ready to introduce the kids to Malcolm."

"Ok. Introduce them," I shrugged.

"You don't think you should meet him first?"

"If you're uncomfortable about it, then maybe it's not time yet. I trust you to make the best decision for our kids. Do your thing." I walked over to the door and held it open for her to leave.

"Damon." She scrunched her lips up. "Men can see things in other men that women can't see. I might be missing something."

"Fine, Vanessa. Set it up. We can do a bar or something."

"No, Damon." Vanessa stopped the door from shutting on her. "You need to give me a date and a time because I don't want you saying you can't make it."

"Ok, Vanessa. Let me look at my schedule. I'll text you tonight."

"I'm serious, Damon." Vanessa didn't bother to look back as she let the screen door shut.

I was just happy for her ass to be gone. She was already fifteen minutes later than she was supposed to be. Cease was dropping the kids off to me, and he usually arrived a little early. All for her to tell me about a fucking Malcolm. I didn't care nothing about that man.

My kids could talk and if something was wrong, they were going to tell me. If I didn't need to whip his ass, we didn't need to meet. I told Neek the same shit about Cease. She wanted me to have a conversation with him, too. We both went to school with the nigga. He had two kids of his own. He knew how this shit worked, and he knew I would fuck him up if he fucked with mine. Cease and I got cool organically. Women always wanted some sit down shit.

It was why I chose to be single. I was actively dating. Every woman I entertained knew that I wasn't looking for a relationship. I wasn't just looking to fuck either. Sometimes, I just wanted the company of a soft ass woman. I was about my children all the time. Everything I did was for them. Their mamas wanted to drop them off unexpectedly; I dropped everything and didn't feel no way about it.

The front door opened, and Tyzee walked in first.

"Hey, dad." He dapped me up and went straight into his room. It wouldn't be long before Nisha was in their making TikToks while he played the game.

"Hi, Daddy." Tynee wrapped her arms around my waist. It took her a long time to warm up to me, but she was my little angel now. Girl never wanted to leave my side, and I loved it.

Cease and I usually did a drop, wave, and go. We hung out from time to time, but that was planned in advance. I didn't know why he was standing in my doorway.

"Go say hi to your sisters, baby girl," I patted her back and she took off up the steps.

"What's up, Cease?" I met him at the door and gave him dap.

"I wanted to talk to you," he scratched the back of his neck.

"About Neek?"

It wouldn't be the first time he wanted my advice on dealing with her extraness. I tried to help as much as I could because I knew he had to humble himself to ask his girlfriend's ex anything. It would never be me, but I supported how much he loved her.

"Yeah and no. It's more about Qualik."

He didn't need to explain any further for me to know exactly what he wanted to talk about. I glanced down at my watch. "That's a big conversation. I tell you what. We'll meet up at the bar this week, and we'll talk."

“Bet. Thank you, man.”

“No problem.” I shut the door behind him.

He was helping me out more than he thought because his ass was coming with me to have this talk with Malcolm. I could kill two birds with one stone, all the while helping both of my baby mothers out.

Sever Days Before Christmas

Elayah

I didn't have the most luxurious job, but I loved it. What I loved most about it was the time it gave me away from the house. It wasn't the family; it was the space. I felt cramped in all the time. It was a big house for a single family. We had a lot of support with the kids, but Cease being on Lik so bad was interrupting our flow. Lik was always in a bad mood; he stayed gone as long as he could to avoid Cease. With us working different shifts, we didn't get much time for us. I knew the time would come, but having our own place would get us more time now not later. I thought I would enjoy a less clingy Lik, but I didn't. I wanted him and my son up under me. The way it was supposed to be. Qua'Layah was a daddy's girl. I lost that battle in the hospital room.

Lik didn't want me working. He wanted to be the sole provider, and I respected it, but it wasn't realistic. The economy was hard as fuck for single people who only had to take care of themselves. These days, two incomes were required to barely float above water. If he wanted to be that type of provider, he would have to get that type of job, which most often required school, at least a semester of classes, and he refused. I had to beg him to let me get this job, and it was only part-time.

I only had an hour left on my shift, so I was going through my checklist for my relief. I heard the front door open and peeked from the kitchen.

"Oh, hey, Griff." I looked down at my Apple Watch. "You're early."

"Yeah, finished my errands and grabbed some food. Didn't

make sense to go all the way home. I'm just gonna eat this food, if you don't mind." He raised his bag.

"Not at all. It smells good. What you got?" I joined him at the table in the dining room.

"Some Lake Trout. You want some?"

"Nah, I'm good. You just gave me a good idea for dinner, though. Thanks." I got up from the table. "If you don't mind, I'm going to head out early since you're here. He shouldn't need anything before your shifts starts." I gave him the run down on the one patient at the house.

"Aw man," he wiped his mouth with a napkin. "I thought I was going to have some company."

"Sorry," I smiled. "Not today. I've been trying to grab these shoes for my son, but I haven't had the time to do anything in stores. I have time to grab a few things if I leave now." I started putting my coat on because whether he said yes or no, I was leaving.

"Alright. I guess I'll see you at the Christmas party?"

"Yep. I grabbed my purse and keys. "I'm still trying to convince Qualik, but I'll definitely be there. See you there." I headed out of the front door.

I wasn't interested in making friends at work, but Griff was cool. He was better than my relief for Saturdays and Sundays. Mrs. Barb was a headache, and she was always late. I wasn't interested in making enemies either. I wanted work to be work, so I killed her with kindness whenever I had the urge to curse her old ass out.

The mall wasn't close to work, but it was five minutes from home. I ended up riding past and going straight in the house because I was tired. I couldn't take my mind off that Lake Trout that Griff had.

"Babe, can we do Lake Trout for dinner? My co-worker had some, and I can still smell it." I moved around the room, gathering my things for a shower.

"Yeah, put in the order. I'll go grab it. You want me to take the kids?"

"Just Quay. You know I can't even breathe alone with him," I laughed.

"Come on, Twin. Mommy said you gotta come with Daddy." Lik grabbed Quay up and put his coat on him. He was holding tight to his tablet. We limited his time on it, but he wasn't going with Lik without it. I had a mama's boy. Two of them.

"Don't tell him that," I sucked my teeth.

"Daddy, I want to go, too," Qua'Layah rushed around to grab her things.

Our space in the attic provided the kids with their own space to sleep and play but somehow, their shit was always in our room.

"Aight, lil' mama, put your coat on."

Qua'layah smiled widely, rushing off the bed from Lik, helping her with her shoe to go with him.

I used that time to take a longer shower. It was a rare thing for me to get a long shower. If it wasn't the kids, it was all the hot water being gone from all the people in this damn house.

Ronika

Cease and I would be kid free, if it weren't for me having Savion. Well, Lik's two were here, but so was Elayah, so I didn't have to worry about them tonight. Shatia helped out a lot, but it was the holiday season, and her schedule was full of appointments. I knew because I couldn't book on her site to get my shit done. She said she would make time to do my hair still, and she always kept her word, so I was just waiting my turn. Rahleigh was being such a bitch lately that I didn't even want to ask her to take Savion off my hands for a few hours. I just wanted a damn nap.

"Baby!" Cease called out as he came down the steps. "You ready?"

"Nooo. I want to sleep," I whined.

"We gotta finish this Christmas shopping." Cease came around the couch and pulled me up. He held me in his arms and rocked me. "How about we give Elayah some money to watch Savion?" he kissed my neck, "we finish this Christmas shopping," he planted another kiss, "and then we get some food?"

"With dessert." I gave him a peck on the lips.

"I was hoping you would be the dessert," he raised his eyebrows.

"Oh, I can get with all of that."

"Don't stop on account of me. I'm just grabbing a new pack of wipes from the kids' pantry." Elayah tried to tip toe by us.

"We'd like to keep the day going if you could keep a certain three-year-old who is currently in our bed on his tablet, for a fee of course."

"A hundred dollars," Elayah held out her hand.

"Girl," I sucked my teeth.

"Ma, I hear you, but it's almost bedtime for my two. Savion goes to sleep when he wants to. And it's Christmas, and I still have gifts to buy."

"Just give it to her, Cease." I rolled my eyes.

"Thank you. Y'all enjoy what's left of the day. Anything after midnight has a hundred dollar fee attached because I worked today, and I work in the morning," she smiled, continuing to the pantry.

Cease and I rushed out of the front door before she could change her mind. Cease got the bright idea to get a room. We were able to put a wrap on our Christmas shopping before we snuck off to the hotel.

We hadn't had sex since before Lik's party. I was stressed from all the running around for him. The argument hadn't made anything better. Cease was for make-up sex, but I wasn't. At this age, those disappointing moments dried my box right on up. It took more than a pitter patter between my legs and some hot wings to get it dripping again.

We stood in the center of the room, kissing. I reached for his dick through his pants, and he pulled away.

"You better get it while the getting is good." I began coming out of my clothes.

"Baby, you look good as fuck." He stood with one hand on his hip and the other scratching his forehead.

"Then come get some."

"I would love to, but this is not for me. This is for you. All day long, all you say is that you need a nap."

"But when you do sweet shit like this, I wanna give you some," I poked my lip out, making Cease laugh.

"We can do that later. For now, you take a nap, and I'm going to do my Christmas shopping for you. I'll be back and when I get back, I expect that ass in the air." He tapped my ass, gave me a kiss on the cheek, and left. I jumped right into bed.

It wasn't always an argument with us. It was just that the shit we were arguing about were my children. More times than not, Cease was catering to my needs. He was gentle, clingy, and protective. Cease was scared of losing me, and that shit felt good. He and Lik were the same person and that was probably why they got into it so much. I'd bow to Cease on anything except my children. I didn't play about my kids. I hoped it wouldn't take us out but if it did, so be it.

I closed my eyes, and all I saw was Rahleigh. Something was going on with my baby. I could feel it in my chest whenever I got a moment of silence. I could hear it in her voice. In Keon's voice. I wanted her to come to me because I didn't know what the situation was and didn't want to make it worse. My approach was still prickly. She'd come to me soon, hopefully.

Keon

I tried to leave the streets alone. I wanted to be one of those black TV dads, I swear it. My heart was ready for that but my mind, what I knew, all I knew was survival. Even with the woman of my dreams in my face, a real career, and on a path of real security, I was still worrying that at any second, it could be taken away from me. I couldn't trust anything good because I didn't know shit else; I knew shit was going to go bad. Not with the hustle, though.

I wasn't one of these niggas who'd been done bad by the streets. I was lucky to have an easy course. Two things always secured me. One, I did my dirt by myself. Two, I had Donjae. Watching Donjae, I learned when it was time to pull back and time to go harder. He paid attention to the signs. Life gave you signs. Like, I knew it was a bad idea to work with Lik because he walked through mud to get to me. He had some heavy shit on his head, and he wasn't thinking straight. He was bound to fuck up. He couldn't be with me when he took that L.

"I'm going to do some Christmas shopping with Shatia. I'll be back in a few."

"Aight. I'll see you," I told Leigh.

"I'll grab food with Sha, so go ahead with dinner. I love you."

"I love you, too."

Signs were saying Rahleigh was cheating. I hated to think about that, but she was hiding something big from me, and it wasn't that shit with my mother. Parts of me felt like she wanted me to break up with her. I guess she didn't want to hurt me. She was already doing that, though.

On top of that, we hadn't had sex in months. Like, nothing. I didn't know how much longer I was going to be able to go without it. Again, I wanted to be that TV black man, but I wasn't there yet. I needed my dick sucked.

"You hungry, ma?" I walked into my mother's room.

"No, I'm good, baby." She smiled at me. "Everything alright?" she examined my face.

"No," I ran my hands down my face, "but I'm going to figure it out."

"You always do."

"Right. I'm fitna run out to our old way to grab some food. I'll be back."

"Ok. Be careful."

"I will, ma." I shut her bedroom door.

All the niggas I knew talked about wanting to take care of their mothers for life. I was one of them. I didn't know it looked like this, though. Like them, I was thinking money. Providing for my mother because the nigga who made me didn't help her. I owed her that. It was so much more than paying a bill or two. This shit was emotional. My mother lost her spunk, she didn't tell jokes anymore. She said the least amount of words as possible. She wouldn't even look me in my eyes anymore. I didn't know what to do with what I was feeling.

These were the moments I was supposed to be able to go to Rahleigh for encouragement, peace, and pussy. It was starting to feel like I was doing life by myself. If that was how it was going to be, then I might as well be by myself. You always hear that women weren't strong enough to leave but neither were men. I wasn't no soft ass nigga, but I'd always been soft on Rocky. That was my baby.

"Aye, let me get uh—"

"Six piece chicken box, salt, pepper, hot sauce on everything, ketchup only on the fries, with a large half and half, and a piece of double chocolate cake." A girl behind me called out my exact order.

I glanced back at her. "Yeah, that."

"Sorry." She bit her lip. "We're just always in here at the same time, and you get the exact same thing every day."

"I ain't never seen you before."

"$10.26!" the clerk called out.

"My bad, Ma," I told the clerk as I passed her the exact amount. If I didn't have to break a bill, I wasn't going to.

"I just moved here about two weeks ago. But you don't live around here." She put her water and hot sausage on the counter. "Can I get a cold cut with everything, no hots. Thank you." She placed a twenty on the counter.

"I used to."

"Where do you live now?" the girl asked, moving to the side and standing in front of me.

"That's a private question," I laughed at her.

"So, you live with your baby mother, mother, or girlfriend. Got it," the girl smirked at me.

"You a trip. What's your name?"

"Beige, but everyone calls me B."

"Cold cut, ready," the cashier called out.

"Nice to meet you, Beige. I'm Key." I put my hand to my chest.

"I know who you are. You the man to see." She walked to the counter to grab her food. I was annoyed that her shit was done first, but it didn't require any heat.

I scrunched my face up. How was a bitch I never met telling me what I did? Nobody knew that shit. At most, some thought I was still hitting houses, but no one knew how I was really moving out here.

She walked out of the store, and I went after her.

"Where you going? You can't say no fly shit like that and walk off. How the fuck you know that?" I asked her.

"Because you can't be a boss in unfamiliar territory and not know who is who. Have a goodnight, Key." She walked off, biting into her hot sausage.

I watched her walk away, and I could feel my dick get hard from her walk alone. I wanted to see what she looked like underneath that coat. I knew I should stay away from her, but she got one up on me. I had to return the favor.

Six Days Before Christmas

Shatia

"Good boy," I coached Yah as he slurped my cum up in front of the fire escape, first thing in the morning.

"Yes, ma'am."

I was using the back of the couch to hold me up with one leg propped on his shoulders. He was on his knees with a face full of my pussy. I was watching the snow fall, and it easily turned a quick fuck into a romantic, messy morning.

"Go get in the bed." I gripped his chin and kissed his lips.

"Yes ma'am." He stood and went into the bedroom.

I came out of the heels I was wearing and followed him into the bedroom. I sat on the bed against the headboard.

"Sit right here," I pointed in between my legs.

Yah Yah was ass naked, sitting in between my legs. I jerked his dick while licking all over his back. He snuggled his mouth into my neck while I stroked him. His soft moans went straight to my ears. I worked my hips against his back, massaging my pussy with the pressure of his body.

"Can I cum, please?" Yah began to beg.

"Not yet. You better hold it."

Yah began flinching and jerking his body around, all the while begging me to let him cum. I finally let him explode in my hand, and the sound he let out had me cumming again.

"Eat it up."

He quickly turned around and dug his tongue inside me

while sucking on my clit. My whole body shook as I came down his throat.

I gripped his chin to pull his body upwards. I brought his lips to mine, and we kissed as he put his dick in me. Yah fucked me slow until I lost count of how many times I came on it.

"You ready to cum?" I asked him.

"Please, ma'am."

I moved from under him and let him lay on his back. I fucked him amazon style. It was my favorite thing to do to him. It allowed him to be all the way in me, rock hard, and his moans were to die for. He would sound like he was crying, but there would be no tears, just the most perfect sex faces. When I saw he was about to cum, I caught it in my mouth. I never thought I'd be that girl, but Yah made me want to go the extra mile to please him the way he pleased me.

This was why I couldn't leave his ass alone. I was having the best sex I'd ever had in my life. This was the sex life everyone dreamed of.

I got off the bed and prepared for a shower.

"Where you going?" Yah asked, sitting on the side of the bed, rubbing through his cruddy.

"Brunch with Israel's family. I thought I told you," I lied. I knew I didn't tell him because it wasn't his business, and I was picking up on some jealousy from him.

"You ain't think you told me shit. You play a lot of games, Shatia."

"What games? We're not together," I shrugged.

"Because you said you didn't want a relationship but yet, you're running off to spend time with Israel's family. Y'all acting like a fucking couple."

"My family will be there, too. We do this every year. I get why you don't understand it, but he's family."

“Family that’s in love with you,” Yah added. “You don’t think my brothers told me everything when they saw I had my eyes on you?”

“Was. He was in love with me. Before, a long time ago. We’re just friends now. But why does it matter? We’re fucking. That’s all we do. You act like we’re in some kind of romance movie where this turns into something more.”

“Why can’t it?” Yah asked.

“You haven’t even asked for it. You told me you love me the other day. Big deal. Of course, we love each other. We’re apart of each other’s families. What you haven’t said is that you want to give this a real go. You just want me because I make you feel good. And that’s fine. No need to complicate things.”

“Shatia, I love you like I don’t want to be without you love you. Like, I don’t want you going to this nigga’s family brunch, love you!”

“Well, that’s the first sign that it’s not going to work out. Israel is a big part of my life. He’s part of the reason you’re in love with me, as you say. I don’t mean to sound harsh, but there’s something he does for me that no one else does. Like, I don’t even know how to explain it. But we are just friends.” I walked into the bathroom and shut the door.

I didn’t want to talk about that anymore. I didn’t want to lose Yah as much as he didn’t want to lose me, but Israel was my person. Life was easier for me with him in my corner.

When I got out of the shower, Yah Yah was gone. I could only hope he would show his face later tonight.

Qualik

We were at Israel's parents' house. We always got together for holidays. Sometimes it was at Ma's, other times at Ms. Letty's. Israel's mom made these fire ass steamed shrimp, and I was always waiting to get my hands on them. Elayah usually went off with Israel's sisters, Egypt and Sahara, but she had to work. I was going to take her a plate later. The kids went to play with the other kids, and I was with Jeru, Keon, and Israel. We were in the backyard, smoking. I ain't have much rap for Keon since he didn't want to put me on with whatever the fuck he was doing.

"Fuck wrong with you, yo?" Keon asked Israel.

I wasn't going to say shit, but Israel was standing there, looking sad as shit.

"Nigga lost his bitch," Jeru laughed.

"Shut your dumb ass up." Israel scrunched his face at his brother.

"Damn, sorry to hear that," I told him.

"He's talking about, Shatia, stupid."

"Nigga, I'll beat your ass out here. Don't be playing with my sister like that," I checked Jeru.

"Chill, chill. I'm just saying. She got somebody else, and this nigga sad as shit about it."

"What you expect, fam? You joined the military, had a whole baby. What she supposed to do?" I threw my arms up, defending my sister.

I thought the both of them were stupid with all that friend shit. They were in love, Shatia was being a scared ass, he left her, and now he lost her. Nigga was stuck in the friend zone, and I didn't feel sorry for his ass.

"Oh, shit," Keon said, as Shatia made her way over to us.

"What's up, sis?!" I called out to her.

"Hey." She gave me a hug and a kiss, before greeting everyone, except Keon, the same. She didn't get too close to Keon since that day he yoked her up. They were cool, though. He just couldn't touch her. "What y'all doing?"

Israel showed her the blunt. "You hitting it?"

"You know I'm not smoking in front of these kids. Y'all shouldn't be either."

"I'm 'bout to head out anyway. I gotta take Elayah a plate before she get to cursing and shit." I gave everybody dap and planted a kiss to Sha's cheek before leaving the smoker's circle.

I didn't have to pack Elayah a plate because Israel's mom already had one with her name written on the bag. I thanked her before driving to Elayah. I didn't have long before someone noticed I left my kids with them. It was just a hassle having to get them in and out of the car. I couldn't wait to be past the booster seat stage.

When I pulled up, I saw some nigga standing on the porch. Elayah said she was taking care of old people, so whoever this nigga was, he had no business being here. He'd had better been a family member of one of the patients.

I left the food on the seat and skipped the front steps two at a time. I tried the knob before knocking, and the door came open. I walked in and Elayah peeked from the kitchen to the door with a face of shock.

"I was just bringing you some lunch," I heard a nigga say.

"Bringing who lunch? Elayah, I swear to God that nigga

better be talking to one of these patients." I moved my hands up and down as I stepped into the kitchen.

"Lik, calm down. This is Griff. Griff, this is my boyfriend, Lik."

"Yeah, nigga. Boyfriend. Elayah what the fuck you got going on?"

"It's not her fault. I was just bringing her some lunch. I didn't think it would be a big deal."

"I wasn't fucking talking to you, bruh."

"Lik, I swear, it's nothing. We just work together." She held one hand to my chest. "Griff, thank you for the food, but I'm in a relationship, and that don't fly with us."

"Understood. I'm sorry."

"Everybody good?" Elayah looked at me.

"Fuck nah, ain't shit good. And you just bought me lunch, nigga." I snatched the bag from his hand.

"Qualik."

"Qualik shit. Get your shit and let's go."

"I can't just leave work, Lik."

I didn't give a fuck about that job. I didn't want her working it anyway. She was going to make me kill one of these overly friendly niggas.

"Well, that nigga gotta get the fuck out. Let's go, yo." I snapped my fingers. I waited by the front door for him to start walking. When he walked by me, I jumped at him. "Bitch ass nigga. You couldn't handle my girl, anyway. Pussy!" I barked in his ear before shutting the door on him.

Elayah shook her head at me.

"Fuck you shaking your head for? I should be shaking mine. You got this lil' nigga pressing up on you and ain't said shit."

“He doesn’t like me, Lik. He’s just a co-worker. We’re cool.”

“I’m not with none of that shit. Elayah, I will shut all this shit the fuck down. Don’t fucking play with me. All that cool shit dead. I’ll see you when you get home.” I shut the door behind myself.

Shatia and Israel were just friends, too. Elayah could get the fuck out my face with that shit. I was the only friend she needed. Cool my ass.

Rahleigh

"You're too far along to still be keeping this a secret from your family. I suggest telling them immediately. You're due any day now, and you're going to need help in that delivery room."

"I hear you, Dr. Johnson."

"See you next time," she smiled, leaving me in the room to get dressed.

I wasn't telling nobody shit. They'd know when my baby was here. All they would do is force me to be excited, and I wasn't.

I chose the latest appointment I could, knowing close to closing would be Keon's busiest time at work. I didn't have to worry about him calling me while at the office. So, when I walked in the house, I was surprised to see him sitting there.

"Where the fuck you been?" I could see the anger in his eyes.

"I was hanging with Shatia," I shrugged.

"That was yesterday. Lie again."

"I'm not lying. Why you not at work? And where's your car? It wasn't out front."

"'Cause I didn't want you to see it. Where the fuck you been, Rahleigh?"

"Minding my business," I spat.

Keon rushed me against the wall. "Stop fucking playing with me." He squeezed my neck.

"I'm pregnant."

Keon's hands immediately let my neck go. His eyes went from cold to curious. He lifted my shirt.

"What the fuck, Rahleigh?" He punched the wall next to my head, and I flinched.

"I was at a doctor's appointment. I'm nine months."

"Who the fuck hides a baby for nine fucking months, yo?!" Keon screamed at me, moving his hands up and down.

"It wasn't hard. You're never home. Who the fuck doesn't notice their girlfriend is pregnant for nine months?!" I yelled back at him.

"A nigga out here making fucking money!" he yelled. "You won't even let me touch you. How was I supposed to notice?"

"Like you have to touch me to notice I'm gaining weight," I shook my head.

"I thought that was some depression shit. I ain't want to make it worse by pointing it out. 'Cause I don't give a fuck how much you weigh. I wasn't going nowhere. I was letting you go through your female shit, and the whole time, you on some trifling shit. All you do is fucking lie, yo."

"And all you do is put everything before me — your mother, work, Jae. I come after everyone."

"You sound fucking stupid. Must be the hormones. I'm gone," Keon shook his head, walking away from me.

"Where the fuck are you going?!" I yelled to the front door that was closing behind Keon.

I followed him outside. He wasn't about to do this shit to me again. He didn't get to leave because I lied. He was going to listen to me. I rushed my pregnant ass out to his car. I banged my fist on the window.

"Get your stupid ass out the car. You not going no fucking where."

Keon finally got out the car, and my fist went into his face.

"Chill the fuck out, Leigh!" He spat into the street and rubbed his jaw.

"You're not fucking leaving. If anyone is leaving, it's me." I swung on him again, but he dodged it and grabbed my wrist. "Get the fuck off of me." I tried to bite his fingers, and he let me go.

"Yo, what the fuck is wrong with you?!" Keon backed away from me.

"You, nigga. You and your mother and this fucking baby that I don't want!"

Keon's eyes watered immediately at my words. He nodded his head.

"Then you should've got a fucking abortion."

Now my eyes were watering. "You don't mean that."

"Go the fuck head, Leigh!" Keon screamed at me before walking towards the house.

I followed him again and began beating on his back. "Tell me you didn't mean that."

"Don't you got somewhere to be? Go!" he pointed to the street.

"Tell me!" I smacked the back of his head.

He turned around fast and glared at me like he was the devil. For the first time, I was scared of him.

"Get your stupid ass in the house." He grabbed my arm and made me get in front of him. "You wearing my fucking patience with this crazy shit. Go the fuck in the house, yo."

I cried, making my way up the steps. I went in the house like he said and waited for him on the couch. I bit my thumb nail while my leg shook out of control. I was prepared to take off after him if he tried to run out of the front door.

He walked into the living room just as I was about to get

up. He sat on the love seat and stared into his phone, completely ignoring me. I didn't care; I just didn't want him to leave.

It wasn't long before our front door opened, and my mother walked in.

"You called my mother?" I was on the verge of tears all over again. I wasn't even ready to tell him. Now, he was forcing me to tell her.

"Yeah, he called me. What the fuck is wrong with you? I swear, if you weren't nine months pregnant, I'd beat your ass all around this fucking house." Tears started spilling from my eyes. "Don't cry now. That shit was plain stupid, Leigh."

This was the exact reaction I expected from her. It would've been the same if she found out when I was in the delivery room. Keon was still sitting there, and that was all I cared about, honestly.

Five Days Before Christmas

Damon

I had Vanessa tell this Malcolm nigga to meet me and Cease at the bar. I gave Cease a time when I dropped the twins off back home. I wanted to get them out the way so I could entertain my favorite woman, the pocket pussy I named Amber. These niggas were getting six minutes of conversation from me, and that was it.

I was disappointed when I saw Malcolm walk in before Cease. I only knew what he looked like because Vanessa insisted on sending me pictures of them out on a date. For her to be wanting me to meet her new man, it felt like she wanted to make me jealous. I had to give a fuck about her first. Outside of my girls, I didn't care nothing 'bout Vanessa. She was a headache that I was glad to have gotten rid of.

"Damon?" Malcolm walked over with his hand out.

"Yeah, man. Nice to meet you." I stood to shake his hand.

"Same, brother, same." He took his leather jacket off while simultaneously ordering a beer from the bartender.

"We're waiting on one more. My other baby mother's boyfriend. He wanted to talk to me, Vanessa wanted us to talk. I figured I could get it all out the way at one time. Hope that's cool." I lied 'cause if I gave a fuck, I would've asked before I did it.

"That's cool with me."

"Oh, there he goes right there." I pointed Cease out as I put my hand up for him to see me.

"What's up, man?" Cease walked over and dapped me.

"Ain't much. Cease, this is Vanessa's boyfriend, Malcolm.

Malcolm, this is Ronika's boyfriend, Cease."

They dapped and exchanged greetings. Cease ordered shots for us all. I wasn't prepared for a long night at the bar but if he was paying, I'd stay a little longer. We took the shots and ended up lost in the game. We were all football fans, so the three of us yelled at the screen in support of our team.

"So, what's going on with Lik?" I asked Cease during a commercial break.

"Man," he shook his head, "he don't want me saying shit to him, so Neek doesn't want me saying anything to him. But the boy needs to grow up. Neek and Elayah do everything for him. They act like he has some kind of disability or something. He's not taking life serious enough, and Neek is fine with it."

"How are the other kids treating you?" I asked.

"Like they want to fight. They don't say shit to me, Damon. Rahleigh is at the house right now." He took a sip of his beer. "Pregnant," he said, tapping my chest.

"Rahleigh is pregnant?" My eyes went wide. The kids hadn't even mentioned it to me. I thought I was done with Christmas shopping; now I had to go back and add things for a baby. The shit was never ending. I hated fucking Christmas.

"Nine months pregnant at that. She been hiding it. Anyway, she walks in the house with Ronika last night and rolls her eyes at me and goes into my fridge. What kind of shit is that?" Malcolm and I laughed. "That shit not funny."

"It don't matter if you pay every bill in that motherfucker, that's they mama house to them. They're like a pack of wolves. They go off on their own from time to time, but they know where home is. If you fuck with one of them, you fuck with all of them. They not gon' deal with you until you work shit out with Lik. Ronika can't even control that."

"So, what I'm supposed to do?" he threw his arms up, "let the nigga be a bum?"

"Yep," I nodded my head. "Or spend the rest of your relationship arguing about him. Lik is her favorite, and they all know it. When it comes to him, she don't have a single hard spot. Let her deal with whatever happens with him. Take yourself out of that. I'm trying to tell you," I shook my head.

"That's all you got? Mind my business?" Cease scrunched his face. "What about you?" Cease looked to Malcolm.

"I don't even have children, my brother. I got nothing for you. Good luck, though," Malcolm laughed.

"No kids?" Something about that bothered me. "Why not, if you don't mind me asking?" A single man with no children should be after a better woman than Vanessa.

"My father has thirteen kids, scattered across three different states. I'm number thirteen. I didn't want that for myself. So, I've wrapped it up every single time. I'm terrified to have children with the wrong woman."

"Smart man," I nodded my head, taking a sip of my beer.

After the game went off, we stuck around and played some pool. Before the night was over, we exchanged numbers with Malcolm, promising to invite him out with us the next time. I hit Vanessa on the ride home, letting her know I was cool with Malcolm meeting the girls. I wasn't sure what she wanted. I could ask him all the questions in the world but he was a man, and we had answers ready. The best way to get to know him was to kick it with him.

Four Days Before Christmas

Elayah

I moved around our bedroom, getting ready for the Christmas party at work. Qualik was sitting on the bed, pretending not to notice me. I hadn't managed to convince him to come to the party and after the last incident at work, I didn't even want to bring it up again.

"Do you need anything before I leave?" I asked him with my car keys in hand, ready to go. "I got six minutes before I have to leave." I looked down at my watch to confirm.

"I been waiting for you to tell me where you're going," Lik said, not taking his eyes off the TV.

"The office Christmas party. I told you about it, and you said you didn't want to go."

"I forgot all about that shit. Usually, you beg me up until the day of. You ain't said shit else about it."

"Why would I when you went off on my coworker the other day? I just want to have a good time. I'm a mother, a girlfriend, an auntie and everything else twenty-four seven. I deserve a night out. I'm lucky I still have a job after the way you showed your ass."

"Nah, you lucky I let you have a job after the way you let that nigga play with me like that. Fuck is you talking 'bout, girl?"

"I know it looks like you can let me do shit, but it don't work like that when you coming up short. When you move us out of here, then you can tell me some shit. I try to keep the peace, but I don't know who the fuck you think you be talking to sometimes. You got one daughter, and her name is not Elayah."

"You talking real fucking spicy. Like I said, I'm gon' let you go to this party, but you better say your goodbyes. You not going back to work. And call my bluff if you want to. I'll blow that fucking office up. Try me."

"How mature," I mumbled, shaking my head and making my way to the front door.

"You think I give a fuck? I'll work two jobs; you can sit your ass in the house with these kids."

I huffed and puffed, walking out of the house. If I said something else, it was going to turn into an argument where he didn't want me going to the party at all. Being with him was frustrating.

I loved my job, and I loved having friends outside of Lik's family. My everyday life was wrapped up in his family. He loved that for us, but I would like a friend to vent to without worrying about my word choice because I was talking about their brother, friend, or son. I still had my brother and grandmother, but the last thing I would do is complain to them about Qualik.

In the office parking lot, I debated on going inside or not. I could go ghost and never talk to any of these people again. It would be less embarrassing than telling them my boyfriend was making me quit. There was a time when I bragged about how overprotective Lik was. More and more, it was starting to look like he was insecure, and it was going against everything I knew him to be.

A tap at my window made me jump out of my seat. I rolled my window down for Griff.

"Hey, I wanted to apologize for the other day. My boyfriend misread the situation and—"

"He didn't misread anything. I'm interested in you."

That was like a slap in the face. Here I was, thinking my man was insecure when he knew exactly what he was talking about. I was still naïve as the day I met him. I felt so stupid.

"You know I have a boyfriend, why would you—"

"I don't care. You deserve—"

"Un unh. That's where you lost me. Qualik and I are not just in a relationship. We are a family. I don't care what it looks like to you, or what made you comfortable enough to try me or my nigga. My home is happy." I rolled my window up and pulled off.

Fuck that party. I was going home to my family. I thought I wanted a life outside of them, but if all I was going to get was fakers and pretenders, I didn't need to be outside. I had real love surrounding me; it was going to have to be enough.

Qualik

"Hey, Qualik, what's up?" Cease walked through the front door.

"'Sup." I stood from the couch. "Time to go upstairs, y'all," I told Qua'layah and Quay.

"Nah, man. They can stay. I wanted to talk to you for a second." Cease cleared his throat.

"I'm not really for all that arguing shit right now. You made it clear you don't like me. I ain't too fond of you. I'm working on getting the fuck out of here. Until then, I'll stay out of the way," I told him.

"You think I don't like you?" Cease scrunched his face up.

"My nigga, you don't. You call everybody else by their nickname, but it's always Qualik with me. What the fuck is friendly about that? You stay on my case about my kids, but don't say shit about Savion pretending to be fucking Spiderman and climbing the walls. My girl gets an attitude, and it's a whole issue but Leigh, Sha, and even Say can say whatever 'round this bitch and nothing. You don't say shit about it, and they don't even live here. You ain't gotta fake the funk for me. Do that shit with my mother." I pointed my finger as I spoke to him.

"I call you by your name because that's the tone you set. From day one—"

"From day one, I welcomed you, nigga. I don't want to hear that shit!" This was why I didn't want to talk to this nigga. He frustrated me with this fake bullshit. Nigga never wanted to keep it real.

"You're right." Cease held his hand out in front of him to calm me, I guess. "You were welcoming. But the day we moved together, blending the families, you stopped respecting me. I don't call you Lik because it feels like I'm crossing a boundary. You set the tone for wherever we are now. But I'm trying to talk, so we can get this shit right for your mother."

"Then get that shit right with her." I held my arm out as my voice went high. "I don't have to be a part of shit y'all got going on. Stop fucking with me."

"I can't do that. When I signed up to be with your mother, all of you were a part of the package. I cannot stand by and watch you take life so lightly. This shit is real, and it's hard as fuck. I'm just trying to make sure you can stand on your own two should something happen to your mother. I'm hard on you the most because you have the heaviest load. No disrespect to Elayah, but Jae has Say. She's as independent and strong willed as your mother. But Elayah..."

"Watch what you say next, Cease."

"Elayah relies on you the way your sisters rely on you and your brother. She can't help you figure it out because she doesn't know herself. You can't fail at life. You're gonna have to go harder. I'm just trying to make sure you're good out here." Cease raised his arms. "That's it. My approach may not be the way, but I've never done this before. I have teenagers. So, my bad if you don't feel respected or liked, but I love you just as much as I love the rest — including my own, Lik."

"We need to talk." Elayah stormed through the front door.

"Go 'head. I can watch the kids for a few," Cease said.

"I gotta go deal with her," I looked at Elayah storming up the steps. "But I hear you. Thank you." I gave him dap before following Elayah up the steps.

I wasn't sure if I could take Cease for his word but for the sake of my mother, I would try.

"I quit my job. Well, not formally or anything, but I'm not going back."

"Good." I shut our bedroom door behind me.

"I didn't do it for you. I did it because you were right about Griff."

"I'll beat that nigga the fuck up."

Elayah rolled her eyes. "Can you listen?" I exhaled and nodded my head. "I do this motherly shit. I'm good at it. I do this wife shit without a ring. I'm okay with both, but I don't want to do it here anymore. I love your mother. I love your entire family, but I want us to be on our own. I want to know what it feels like. I want to make the rules instead of following them. So, I'm going back to school. I want to be a postpartum doula. It's going to take about two years. We're going to need the support so we can put moving on the back burner for now, assuming that you stop threatening Cease," she rolled her eyes.

"Cease and I are good."

"Ok. I love that you want to be everything for me and the kids, but I want to do my part. I don't want to be another weight on your shoulders."

"Whatever you want, baby. It's your world. I'm just living in it."

We hugged tightly before kissing aggressively. It would've led to sex if my phone didn't ring. I saw Jeru was calling. This nigga would call when I wasn't in a bind no more.

"Hello?" I answered, while Elayah's nosey ass stared in my face.

"Yooooo. You ready?"

"Um, yeah. But what we doing?"

"I'll tell you when I get there. I'm on my way."

"Aight." I ended the call. I moved to the closet and tossed my black hoodie over my head.

"Where you going?" Elayah was already pouting, and I didn't even get the chance to answer her question yet. I put my Skully on, in case whatever we were doing required it.

"I gotta go handle something with Jeru. I won't be long. Promise."

"Be safe, Lik."

"I will. I'm coming home. I said I promise." I gave her a kiss, before leaving out of our bedroom.

I made promises for myself. If I gave my word, I knew I would try to keep it. It ain't matter what happened; I was coming back home. Riding with Jeru sounded good when I was desperate. But now, the shit had my stomach turning.

Donjae

I was ready to go home. Tasaya was having the time of her life, though. I chose to fake the funk so I didn't ruin her good time. I was on edge about Jeru picking up the work from Santi. I gave Santi a heads up, but my mind wasn't settling. That only happened when I was moving wrong. I was trying to push through and focus on our anniversary for Say Say. I hated keeping this from her because she was legit my best friend. She could talk me through hell if I needed her to.

"Baby, I think we're going to need another suitcase to get all this stuff back home." She was holding the door for me to get in our room with all of her bags.

I was her assistant by day and her plumber by night. Sometimes, I did some plumbing in the morning, too.

"We don't need anything. That's you, shopping like you need a new wardrobe."

"What's even crazier is that I'm really going to need a new wardrobe in a few weeks."

"Say." I looked at her with my face twisted up as I put the bags down.

"What?" she whined and shrugged her shoulders.

"You do too much," I shook my head.

"Well, I mean, we're having a baby, so I can't wear the shit I wear now. It's messed up, too because I worked hard to get my body back, and I'm going to have to start all over again," she shook her head.

"Let's save the shopping until we get a positive pregnancy test." She was always jumping the gun. I said I was trying to have another baby a few days ago, and she was running with it. I loved her dedication, but she was always doing the most.

"You so slow," she shook her head. "Baby, I'm already pregnant," Say laughed. "I took the test this morning." She came over to me and held my face. "We're having a baby," she hugged me.

My mind raced. This was what I wanted. More love and more kids. My thoughts weren't on that, though; they were on Jeru. It felt like I was risking it all. I looked down at my watch. Jeru should've already been on his way to meet with Santi.

"I need to call Keon." I moved her out of the way and grabbed my phone.

"I just told you that we're having a baby," she brought her arm down and slapped her leg, "and your first thought is to call Keon? Your mom I get, but Keon can wait," Say scrunched her face.

"Say, please."

She snatched my phone from my hand. "You got me fucked up, Jae. Hell no. Your little bromance can wait until we get back home."

"It's serious, Say. Please." I dropped my arms down to my side and gave a long, low sigh.

I watched Say's eyes try and get a read on me. "What are you not telling me?" She swallowed hard and that alone made guilt hit my chest.

"I'm sorry, Say." I ran my hands down my face.

"Stop fucking apologizing and tell me what you did." Her eyes began to water. "You cheated?"

"Hell no!" I was offended at the suggestion. "I'm still in the streets. I'm the plug now." Say's mouth dropped at my confession. "I get the work from Santi and drop it to Jeru. It's just me and him, and nobody else knows. I pick up on Sundays. I'm here, he's there, so I sent him, and I feel like something is going to go—"

"Jeru?!" Say yelled. "You so fucking stupid." Say handed me my phone and walked out of the room.

I hurried to call Keon because I had to catch up to her.

Keon

Shit was all bad between me and Leigh. She was still at her mother's and begging to come back home, but I ain't want to look at her ass. One of us had to be here to look after my mother, and I couldn't trust her to do it so for now, she had to stay where she was. Ma Neek and I texted throughout the day, though. So, I knew she was good— well, as good as she could be when I wasn't fucking with her.

I wasn't getting no peace, though. I couldn't figure out how I missed a whole pregnancy. More than that, it hurt that she took that experience from me. Then, to hear her say she didn't want my baby. Like, women were pure evil. How was I supposed to forgive that? But I'd be expected to because I was the man. I wasn't supposed to let the hurtful shit she said faze me. It was bullshit.

I watched my phone ring with Lik's name and thought about not answering. Lik only called me for two things. He either needed something or wanted to be in me and Rahleigh's business. He hadn't been in our business lately, so that meant he needed something. The phone stopped ringing before I could answer. I felt I dodged bullet until he was calling again.

"Yeah, Lik," I cleared my throat, "what's up?"

"Nigga, don't be answering the phone like I'm bothering you."

"What you want, nigga?"

"I need you on standby. I done got myself into some dumb ass shit with Jeru. I might need you."

"Where y'all at?"

"He fitna pick me up. I don't know where we going or what we doing. But you know this nigga be on dumb shit. My stomach turning. I know the shit ain't right."

"So, don't go, nigga. You acting like you got to get in the car."

"I asked this nigga to put me on; he came through. This your fault really because if you wasn't—"

I hung up the phone and texted him that I was on standby. I ain't feel like hearing that shit. He and Leigh blamed everything on everyone else. I wasn't listening to the bullshit he was talking, but if he needed me, I'd be there.

I was finishing up on a car that needed new brakes. They told me the owner would be picking the car up before closing, but that never happened. It worked out because I didn't start until after closing. I didn't know what happened with them, but they could pick it up in the morning, assuming Lik didn't end up needing me.

"Good evening." I turned around to see the girl who knew too much of my business, Beige.

"Yo," I shook my head. "What you want? How I ain't ever seen you before but you keep popping up? How can I help you?" I asked, frustrated.

"Just coming to pick my car up," she threw her arms up. "Who pissed you off?"

"You, the fuck." I tossed her the keys. "Take your shit and go about your business."

"You can't be the same Key that I heard about."

"You still ain't told me what you heard, so I don't have no rap." I glanced at my phone to see if I had anything from Lik.

"I heard you the nigga to see if I need something big," she smirked. I held my composure. "Said you can get me anything I need." She walked towards me. "I was told to be careful with you because you're charming as fuck and ya bitch fights 'bout you."

"Ha," I laughed. "They told you wrong. My lady fucks shit up about me." I walked to the end of the garage. "I don't really like your energy. Your whole everything," I moved my hand up and down the length of her body, "is off. I'm 'bout my paper, though. So, what you need?"

"A gun. A big one."

I nodded my head. "Three days." I turned to face her. "And I ain't cheap."

"I ain't broke," she shrugged.

"Forty-five hundred. As is, no questions asked."

"I'm not concerned about the bodies on it. Just make sure no one comes looking for it."

"You make sure they don't catch you with it."

She got in the car and pulled off. Beige reminded me of Say Say. She wasn't my type. I liked a woman who was aggressive with other niggas, not me. I wanted softness when I got in from these streets, not a bitch tryna compete. Plus, a bitch like that was already somebody's headache.

My phone rang, and I rushed to it, hoping it wasn't Lik but prepared if it was. Instead, it was Donjae. That nigga wasn't supposed to be calling me. Tasaya had us on some no contact shit until he got home. I was respecting it.

"Yo?" I answered.

"I'm in some shit. I need you, yo." Jae's voice sounded panicked.

"How you get in some shit all the way in Bali, nigga? What the fuck I'm supposed to do?"

"I'm the plug, yo. I got Jeru picking up the work from Santi because I'm all the way out here. The shit don't feel—"

"I just talked to Lik, he with him." I was already locking the garage up to get in my car.

"Go get my brother, yo. If you can stop Jeru from some stupid shit, good look, but get my brother, yo, please."

"I'm already on the way."

I jumped in the car and sped off for Santi's apartment building. I couldn't do too much because I didn't need the boys pulling me over. Then, I'd never get to Lik in time. None of us were sure that Lik needed saving, but both of them were worried, so I was, too.

I could hear shots going off from three blocks away. I ignored the red lights and the stop signs to pull onto the block. I grabbed my gun from the armrest, speeding through, looking for Lik. I didn't see him on my first ride through. I bust a U at the end of the street and sped through again. I could see Lik turning the corner at the end of the street. I stepped on the gas, bending the corner.

"Lik!" I put the car in park to open the passenger door.

He jumped in, and I sped off. "What the fuck happened?"

"Nigga!" Lik tried to catch his breath. "This nigga Jeru picks me up. I straight ask him where we going, what we doing. Nigga not being direct at all. He just kept saying, 'Jae about to own the block, Jae about to own the block'"

"Fuck that mean?" I asked him, slowing my speed down since we were far enough away.

"I ain't know what that shit meant until we met with Santi. This dumb ass nigga tried to rob the connect! Santi gon' kill me, man." Lik put his hand on his head.

"We gon' have to kill that nigga first."

"How the fuck we gon' do that? He got all the guns, all the soldiers. All we got is our fucking name. Fuck we gon' do with that in a gun fight?"

"What else we gon' do, nigga? Go knock on his door and tell him you ain't have shit to do with that? Would you be tryna hear that shit, my nigga?"

"Fuck!" Lik punched the dashboard.

"Yeah, nigga. Fuck!" I nodded my head.

I tried to call Jae, but he didn't answer.

"Go black."

"Black? Nigga, we ain't talked to Jae yet! Fuck you mean, go black?" Lik scrunched his face.

"He'll know something is wrong when he sees we went black. Just do it, damn."

Going black was airplane mode. No location, no contact, just dead. I hoped Jae not answering meant his ass was on a plane home because if Santi wanted Lik, he wanted me and Jae, too.

Tasaya

When I left our room, I didn't have a destination in mind. I only wanted to get away from him before I fucked his stupid ass up. I found myself at the airport, changing his flight. He would be mad that I wasn't going home with him. I would've gone with no hesitation before I found out he was a liar.

It wasn't like I expected him to be perfect. You could've never told me he would fuck up so big and so soon after we exchanged our I dos.

I specifically told him that I didn't want to raise my children in that lifestyle. He argued that he would always keep them away from it. I grew up in that and knew that wasn't a thing. It sounded good, but it was impossible to do.

If you were in the streets, your children were going to feel it in some kind of way. They were going to see it, hear it, or not get much of you as a parent. The streets came with big Ls and little Ls. Your mind was always in a paranoid state of being prepared for whatever, and that mood carried over into the home.

So, when we found out I was pregnant with Savion, Donjae vowed to leave the streets alone. I believed him. Jae hadn't shown so much of an inkling that he still had a toe in that shit. To hear that he never left, broke my heart. What else was he lying to me about?

I expected to see Jae when I walked into our suite, but he wasn't where I left him. I went into our room and found him lying on the bed. He was on his back with his hands folded across his chest. Jae sat up quickly at the sight of me.

"Your flight leaves in three hours." I moved like wind to the closet and pulled out his suitcase.

He wanted to live out of his luggage for the week, but I protested and put his shit away like we lived here. Now that I had to pull all of that shit out of the closet, I wish I would've listened.

"You that mad you just gon' say fuck our vacation?"

"No. I'm that mad, I'm saying fuck you. I'm staying here and enjoying the rest of my trip. You can go home and handle your business." I stuffed his clothes into the suitcase.

Even in my anger, I knew he had to go handle home. Too much could go wrong with Jeru running things in his absence.

"Say say," Jae shook his head. "You got me fucked up."

"Since you wanted to be in business by yourself, you can go handle it by yourself. I'm staying. I'm not the liar. You are. Why should I be punished?"

"We not gon' talk about it or nothing?" Jae looked at me sideways.

"Tuh!" I laughed. "You don't want to hear what I have to say right now."

"I do."

"Ain't shit special about you," I glared at him. "You the same lying ass nigga my daddy is. Lying to me the same way my brothers lie to their bitches. I don't fuck with that. I don't fuck with you."

"One mistake in all these years, and it's fuck me? Just like that." Jae talked with his hands.

"Savion is three. You've been lying to me for three years, Jae, it wasn't one mistake. And nothing about it was a mistake. You knew exactly what you were doing when you decided to keep it from me."

"I never intended to go this long or keep it from you this

long. Shit happens, Say."

"That's a nigga's favorite line. You made this shit happen. You so pressed about being that nigga to the hood instead of being that nigga to me and your son."

"And what about our son?"

"What the fuck are you talking 'bout, Jae?" I scrunched my face, irritated. "You wasn't thinking 'bout him when you did what you did!"

"I was!" He stood off the bed. "I think about y'all so much, I'm in the fucking future wit' it. If for any reason this General Contracting shit fall through, or it ain't enough, or my wife wants to go to fucking Bali, I need my name to hold the same weight in the streets. I don't ever want to be in the position where I have to prove myself again! I need to be able to jump in and out as needed."

"We'll talk about it when I get home."

"So, you are coming home?"

"Duh, Jae." I sucked my teeth and slapped my thigh. "Go 'head before you miss your flight," I rolled my eyes, going into the bathroom.

I saw his vision. I understood his why. It didn't change the fact that he made a whole plan that didn't include me. It felt like the shit with my dad and brothers all over again. I finally moved past it and forgave them but now, I was hurt all over again. I went and picked a nigga just like them. I told Jae what they did to me. How could he do that to me? I never could've done that to him.

Three Days Before Christmas

Shatia

It was my last meeting with Dr. Newson before she went on vacation. Last week, we discussed skipping over this session. I didn't think it would make much of a difference. That was before Israel got home and Yah confessed his love for me. Not only could I not miss this appointment, but I needed at least four drinks.

"Hey, Dr. Newson," I walked into her office. "My life is falling apart," I exhaled, plopping down in the seat in front of her desk.

She twisted her neck at me. "I'm sure not that much has changed in a week, Shatia. Dial it back a notch or two. What's going on?"

"I told you Israel was coming home."

"Yes. You also said that you missed him. So, how did that go?"

"I tried to avoid him until he showed up at my house. I don't know, he said it's no pressure but that's all I've felt since he got home. He and Israel both say they don't want relationships."

"And why don't you believe them?"

"It's no way I feel what they feel, too and neither of them wants a relationship from me."

"It sounds like you want the relationship."

"I don't. I want to keep fucking Yah Yah and keep being best friends with Israel and not lose either of them in the process."

"So, do that," she shrugged, "it sounds like they're not making you choose. You're the only one applying pressure here."

"I'm not!" I snapped. "They're just not saying. I feel it

whenever I'm with one of them. They want me to themselves. They just think they're going to manipulate me into it is all."

"Then don't be manipulated. Shatia, you already know how to handle this. If you don't start trusting yourself, you'll be stuck in this process forever."

This is what the fuck I was saying about her. She wasn't any damn help. I was worse off than before I came in. I had better conversations with the mirror.

I switched to talking about how frustrating my clients were. I was done with giving this bitch my tea if she wasn't going to help me.

On the ride home, Yah Yah called me. I put my AirPod in before answering. I always heard other people's conversations when they talked through the car sync, and I couldn't get with it. I liked my conversations private.

"Hello?"

"How was your crazy people session?" Yah asked. I couldn't help but laugh with him.

"I'm not crazy, asshole."

"You something. How was it though? You feeling good?"

"I am. What's going on with you?"

"Tryna do this nine to five thing." He let out a deep breath.

Tasaya made Yah promise to be legit while in Maryland. I didn't know if he was completely legit, but I saw him trying. He hadn't missed a day and let him tell it, he was only late on mornings he left from my house.

Israel beeped through my line, and I let it ring. I would call him back once I was settled in my apartment. I'd gotten used to my conversations with Yah after my appointments. Israel called again.

"Israel's calling. Let me call you right back," I said to Yah.

"I know you not bumping me back to talk to that nigga."

"I ignored the first call, but he's calling again. Something might be wrong with Zamia. I'll call you back."

"Aight."

I wanted to hang up without explaining, but Yah insisted that calls were ended properly with a farewell of some kind.

"Hello?" I answered Israel's call.

"Sha," I could hear pain in his voice. "They took..." his voice trailed.

"They took what, Israel? I can't hear you." He was fucking with my anxiety. My heart was beating through my chest, and I didn't even know what was wrong yet. "Israel!" I could hear him crying. "I'm on my way." Israel didn't hang up, so I didn't either. "I need you to tell me where you are." I took a shot at getting a response from him.

"Mommy's," he said, barely above a whisper.

"I'm coming."

My mind raced with what could be wrong as I whipped through the streets to get to Israel's mom's house. I loved his entire family. So, every time I had a hope that it wasn't one person, I thought of another I hoped it wasn't.

I was a careful driver, never going above five miles over the speed limit. I stopped at yellow lights and while the cars behind me hated it, I knew I was driving my safest. That wasn't the case today. I needed to get to my best friend.

When I pulled up in front of his mom's, I saw that my mom was already there. Ma was managing my anxiety well. She wasn't going to tell me bad news over the phone because she didn't want me to have a panic attack wherever I was. So, it didn't surprise me that she knew what was going on and didn't call me.

"Whatever it is, it's not going to kill you," I said aloud to myself, getting out of the car.

It was something I learned to tell myself to deal with pain and all the things out of my control. It might not feel good, I might hate it, but it wasn't going to kill me.

I could hear the crying as I walked up the steps. My hands shook so bad, I had to hold right to the railing. On the porch, the front door was wide open, as if we were in the middle of summer instead of winter. I opened the screen door and walked into Israel's home.

Ma was hugging his mom. His dad was being loved on by his grandmother. Sahara was on the couch under Israel's arm. Egypt was moving around, cleaning shit that didn't need to be cleaned. She had anxiety like me.

I looked to my mother, and she nodded her head to confirm the obvious. Jeru was dead. I was overwhelmed. "I'll be right back," I said to anyone listening.

I stood on the front porch and let the tears fall. My problem was that when things like this happened, I imagined it happening to me. The thought of me losing one of my brothers had me crying uncontrollably in my hands.

My phone rang with Yah Yah's number. I pressed ignore and put my phone on do not disturb. But damn if I didn't want to answer it. I know I was supposed to be showing up for Israel, but Jeru was like my brother, too. I was hurt about that shit. Yah would get me together. I sent him a text that I couldn't talk but would need him later.

I whipped my neck around, hearing the screen door open. Israel wiped his hands down his face. I immediately hugged him.

"I'm so sorry," I held on to the back of his neck as he cried into mine.

"I-I-..." Israel never finished his sentence. Israel released me from the hug. He ran his hands down his face. "I gotta get outta here."

"Where you going?"

"I don't know, anywhere but here." He walked down the front steps.

"I'm coming with you." I tried to follow him.

"Thank you, but if you could keep Zakia for me. She's napping on the floor of her playroom."

"Ok." I nodded my head as I watched him continue down the steps. "I love you."

"I love you, too, Sha."

I went back inside, and everyone was exactly how I left them; only, Sahara was holding onto a couch pillow instead of Israel. Egypt was on her knees, cleaning the coffee table. I got down there with her on the other side of the table and grabbed a rag to help her. When I noticed she was cleaning her tears from the table, I was crying all over again.

Ronika

I spent most of my day at Letty's. Charlotte was going through it and while I didn't know what it felt like to lose a child, I had been in this situation before. When Damon and Vanessa lost their son, Tykee and I showed up every day for them. Like them, this was our second family, and I was hurting with them. Jeru was the wildest of all the kids, but it didn't change our love for him. He was family.

After Shatia and I made dinner for the family, we cleaned up and left together. I followed her to her apartment in my car because I wanted to make sure she got home safe. She'd been better managing her anxiety but for my peace of mind, I had to make sure she got home safe. Lord knows if something happened to mine, they might as well toss me on in the casket with them.

Damon called me while I was driving back home. The twins came home on Sunday, but Tyzee asked to go back over to his dad's. They were on Christmas break and since Damon didn't mind, I didn't either. I let him know what was going on and had him break it to Zee. I was headed home to break the news to Tynee.

"Hello?" I answered on the car sync. "Hey. Did you talk to Zee?" I asked him.

"I did."

"Well, how'd it go?" I was trying to see if I needed to rush over there and pick my baby up. Daddies were great but nothing like a mother's comfort.

"He didn't cry if that's what you mean, but he's angry. The first question he asked was who did it. I told him I didn't know, and he shook his head and went up to his bedroom."

"And you just let him go? He has to feel it. With social media and these video games, it makes it easy for these kids to overlook death. I don't want my babies numb to that. I want them to feel it."

"Neek, what was I supposed to do? The boy is allowed to grieve how he chooses. He wanted to be alone. That's the problem with women. Always want a nigga to talk and express himself. He don't feel like talking."

"How did we go from being concerned for our son to you venting about your female issues?" I asked, backing into the driveway of my house.

"Because you questioning me about letting him go to his room as if I was supposed to make him sit here until he started crying or something. He's pissed off, but he's fine."

"Bye, Damon." I hung up on him.

If that man felt the smallest hint of you telling him he was a bad father, he was ready for war, and I didn't have time to go back and forth with him. I had to talk to Qualik. I called his phone because I wanted this to be a private conversation. I was expecting the phone to ring, but it went straight to voicemail. I called Elayah's phone.

"Hello?" she answered.

"Tell Lik to come help me with these bags."

"Ok. I'll throw on some shoes and help, too."

"No, baby. It's not enough bags for that. Just send him. That's what men are for." We both laughed before I hung up, waiting for my son to get to the car.

I hoped I wasn't going to have to put my hands on him, but if I felt he was lying even just a little bit, I was going across his head.

"Where the bags?" Lik pulled the passenger door open.

"Get your ass in this car."

"What I do?" He scrunched his face up.

"I said get your ass in this car."

He exhaled and sat in the passenger seat.

"You know where I been all morning?" I asked him.

"Cease said you was hanging out with Ms. Letty and shit," he shrugged.

"Hanging out? That woman is grieving. The whole family is. You know Jeru got killed?" I looked in his eyes for a lie, but his mouth dropped.

"Nah." He looked out the window.

"Ok, but you knew he got shot?"

Lik's head whipped around like I told his secret.

"Hell no! Yeah, but nah. Some shit went down. I got the fuck outta there. But my phone is off, and I didn't know if he got hit or not.

"What the fuck were y'all doing, Lik? I done sat up under that family all day, waiting for your scrawny ass to walk to that door to pay your respects, and you been in the house doing what all day? Playing that damn game, prolly." I smacked his arm.

"I said I didn't know. I didn't." He put his hand to his head and exhaled. "I been trying to move my family up out of here. I went to Jeru. He called me and said he had a job. I ain't know what the shit was. Come to find out..." He stopped talking like he was about to tell too much truth.

"And what?"

"Basically, that nigga tried to rob the connect, Mommy. I don't know what the fuck he was thinking. I ain't know that nigga was dead though. I assumed he took off the same way I did. I had to get home to my kids. I swear I would've never left him." Lik looked at me with watering eyes.

I exhaled. Jeru was so unpredictable. While I felt for his

mother, I couldn't help but to feel relieved, knowing that my baby was there, and he made it home.

"I'm glad you got out of there."

Lik nodded his head, looking out of the window. "Me too."

"But first thing in the morning, you are going over to that house and telling that woman everything."

I'd never lost a child. But I'd lost a husband. The one question I still had was why him? Lik could give that woman a why, and it would lend her some peace.

"You know I can't do that." Lik was almost out of his seat.

"You can and you will. Boy, ain't nobody asking you to talk to the police. But you gon' give that lady some peace. Shouldn't have had your stupid ass over there doing nothing illegal with Jeru, of all people. First thing in the morning, Lik. I'm not playing with you.

"Aight, man," he shook his head, opening the car door.

"Aye, I love you. I'm glad you made it home."

"I love you, too." He got out of the car.

They say the older they get, the easier it gets, but that was a damn lie. I worried about them more now than I did before. The mess they found themselves in as adults could ruin the rest of their lives. Lik could've been the one killed or mistaken for the shooter. He had to make better choices. Once upon a time, I may have let him slide. But some of the things Cease was saying to me was getting through. I wanted Lik to be more mindful of the shit he did, so he was going to have to bite the bullet on this one.

I stayed in my car for a few minutes longer. I wanted to have my thoughts together for Tynee. The twins never had to deal with the death of a loved one. I mean Tykee, but they were babies. They didn't feel it like they would feel Jeru's death. This was harder than the Christmas we had five years ago. I was going to need at least four drinks — one for Rahleigh, one for Lik, one for Jesus's birthday, and one for myself.

Two Days Before Christmas

Qualik

I was sitting on the couch, with Qua'layah right under my arm on her tablet. Quay and Savion were doing everything but sitting the fuck down. Elayah and Rahleigh were giggling about everything in the world. Every now and then, they would show me shit on their phones that I pretended was funny so they would leave me the fuck alone. I know we were in black mode, but I was fitna jump in the car and head to Keon's to tell him come get his girl. Elayah was definitely right about the house being crowded. I had to get us out of here.

It felt like everyone was acting like Jeru didn't die or that they didn't care. The nigga was reckless, but he was family. That shit hurt. Add to the fact that I was there and left. I felt fucked up about it. Mommy wanted me to go to Ms. Letty's and tell her what happened like that was going to bring her peace. That lady was going to want me dead. I would if I was her. I already had Santi on my head. It wasn't no proof of it, but I knew.

The front door opened, and we all turned to see Jae, Keon, and Say's brothers.

"Jae!" Rahleigh wanted to jump up, but her stomach was in the way, so she stretched her arms out to him.

"The fuck?" He looked back at Keon. "I wasn't gone long enough for you to look like you're ready to drop a baby any day now."

"Her goofy ass was hiding it." Keon shook his head.

"For what?" Jae looked at her sideways before shaking his head.

Everyone greeted each other. It took Savion a few to realize his father was standing in front of him. When he looked up, a smile spread across his face as he hugged Jae's legs. Jae scooped him up and kissed him.

"I missed you, man. You been being good?"

"Fuck no. You need to put that little nigga in some kind of class so he can burn all that energy off." I shook my head.

"I burn you!" Savion yelled at me.

"See." I shook my head while everyone laughed.

"Where mommy?" Savion looked around the room. "She not back yet. She be home soon, ok?"

"Yeah."

"Keon, can we talk?" Rahleigh asked, making shit awkward.

"When I get back. I got shit to handle. I can't think about that right now."

"Daddy be back, okay?" Jae put Savion down. "Come on, Lik."

"You ain't said shit but a word." I stood, sliding my foot into my slides. Jae waited until I pulled my hoodie over my head to tell me that slides weren't going to do it. I ran upstairs to get my sneakers, and mommy was at the top of the steps.

"What's all that noise?" she walked down the steps. "My baby." I could hear the smile in her voice. "I thought you had a few more days."

I grabbed my shoes and came back down to Mommy hugging Jae and the rest of them. I put my shoes on at the bottom step.

"Something came up."

Mommy looked around at us. We were all dressed in all black — black hoodie, black jeans, black skullies.

"Mmm. All I know is, all six of you better make it home. And before y'all do anything, Lik needs to take his ass to Letty's house and tell that woman what happened to her son."

I exhaled, getting off the step.

"Aight, Mama. That's our first stop."

"It better be. Be safe," she told us.

"Yes Ma'am," we all said at the same time.

I rushed over to kiss my kids and Elayah goodbye. "We need you here," Elayah whispered in my ear.

"I know. That's why I gotta do this. I love you."

"I love you, too, baby."

We all piled into Rowdy's black on black Armada. Rowdy pulled out of the space.

"Man, what the fuck I'm supposed to say to this lady?" I said aloud from the back.

"The truth," Donjae answered.

"Man, that lady know what type of time her son be on," Rowdy interjected. "I ain't saying he deserved it, but he knew the risk he was taking."

"And after you tell her that, you tell her we gon' make it right," Rolla said from the front passenger seat.

"I don't know what his stupid ass was thinking," Keon shook his head.

"He was thinking about the come up. I ain't been here that long, and I can see that nigga Santi got this shit tied up. He own everything." Yah was rolling a blunt in the seat across from Jae. "Nigga did that shit all wrong though. I didn't fuck with the nigga, but if he came to y'all with a solid plan or even just the idea, I would've stood then toes downith my brothers." He sealed the end of the blunt paper.

"That's on me. Nigga was wild as fuck, but he was solid. I told him not to tell nobody, and he didn't. We been doing this shit smooth for years, and I don't know why that nigga went rogue like that." Jae ran his hands down his face.

"Speaking of, that was some fucked up shit," Rolla told him.

"It wasn't about none of y'all forreal. Y'all know how Say feel about this shit now."

"She don't want none of us doing nothing even slightly illegal," Keon chimed in.

"Exactly. I figured the more of us doing it, the easier it would be for her to find out. We too comfortable around her. It was hard enough for me to keep it from her. Jeru was scared of her; I knew he wasn't going to let it slip."

"And he didn't," Rowdy agreed. "I ain't mad about it. I kind of like being legit."

"It wasn't easy keeping it from y'all niggas either. Everybody was doing good. I ain't want to stir the pot."

"We get it, nigga. You ain't want Say to fuck you up." Yah had all of us laughing.

"Man, I would've rather she did that. The words she gave me was worse. She changed my flight, packed my suitcase, and sent me on my fucking way," Jae laughed. "I'ma be kissing ass forever behind this shit."

I didn't realize we were at Ms. Letty's house until everyone started getting out the car — everyone except Yah. I thought I was going to have to do this shit by myself. It felt good to have my brothers with me.

"Yah, come on," Rowdy told him.

"I think it would be phony of me to go in that man's house when I didn't fuck with him."

"That nigga dead. That shit don't matter. We gon' show this woman that she can believe Lik when he say we gon' make it right."

"Whatever, man," Yah exhaled, getting out of the truck.

Donjae

Their sister, Sahara, answered the door. "It's about time y'all came to pay your respects," she rolled her eyes, letting us in.

Sahara was rude all the time. She ain't mean no harm. Say and I had had a bet going. She thought Sahara was a closeted lesbian. I knew she was bi because she was helping Jeru move his work. I couldn't tell Say that though. I kept the bet low to be fair. It was all my money anyway.

"Who is it, Sahara?" Ms. Letty asked.

Egypt stepped in the entryway of the kitchen and immediately hid herself. She had a crush on Rowdy and anxiety like Shatia.

"How you doing, Ms. Letty?" I called out to her.

She showed herself in the entryway and made her way to us. She hugged all of us, even Yah.

"I'm doing the best I can. Better than this morning, but it'll go to shit soon, I'm sure."

"We're sorry for your loss," Rowdy told her.

"Yeah," Rolla cleared his throat. "We ain't know him well, but anybody who's family to the Carterets are family to us, too," Rolla nodded his head.

"I appreciate that. Y'all want some food or something? People keep bringing me this mess." She turned to the kitchen.

"No. We're not staying long. Thank you, though," Keon added.

"Ms. Letty," Qualik stepped forward. "I know what happened to Jeru."

She stopped where she was.

"You should've fucking led with that." Sahara got up from her seat, walking over to us.

"Sahara, shut the fuck up." Ms. Letty walked over to us. "So, what did he do? I know my son, and I know the shit he gets himself into."

"He tried to rob the connect," Lik told her.

I was proud of him. I was fully prepared to have to take his place and tell Ms. Letty what happened.

She gave a small laugh of disbelief. "That was my Jeru. Eyes always on the prize. Thank you, Qualik. I know that wasn't easy for you, but it made it easier for me to know the why." She hugged him.

"You're welcome."

I cleared my throat. "We fully intend to make this right."

"I want his head on a fucking pole," she said as calmly as announcing she was going to take a nap. "Thank you for coming." She walked off up the steps.

"I want in," Sahara told us once her mother was gone.

"Sahara, go the fuck head somewhere," Keon told her as we walked out of the house.

"I'm serious," she begged. "It was my brother."

"He was our brother, too," Lik told her.

"We got it," Rolla told her.

"We take you out there with us and something happens to you, we gotta come back and do this all over again." I put my hand on her shoulder. "Take care of your mother and sister."

Her eyes watered and she nodded her head. "Thank y'all. I

love y'all," she wiped her eyes.

"We love you, too," Keon told her as we left the house.

We piled back in Rowdy's truck.

"I know we got to get this shit figured out, but y'all know I can't do all that killing on an empty stomach."

"Nigga, you can't do shit on an empty stomach, damn," Yah told him, and we laughed.

"I could go for some food," I chimed in.

"Waffle House it is," Rowdy said.

"How the fuck you niggas tryna sit in a public ass restaurant when niggas got money on their head? You niggas is on some bullshit. Take me the fuck home. Get me when y'all ready to dead some shit," Lik went off.

"Boy, ain't no money on your head," Yah told him.

"Santi seen me, nigga. I know it's money on my shit!"

That was confirmation for me that Lik was scared. He ain't ever been that close to some shit like that before. Lik never had to own a gun, let alone kill someone. Our name kept us untouched, but this was some different shit.

"Ain't no money on your fucking head!" Yah yelled. "It's money on Jae's head, not yours," Yah confessed.

"And when the fuck was you gon' tell niggas that?" I asked.

I wasn't worried; I figured as much but for Yah to be sitting on that information irritated me.

"We going to dead that nigga and his whole camp. Fuck it matter for?" Yah shrugged, and he sealed another blunt. "If it's that serious, it's money on Keon, too."

"Nigga," Keon threw his arms up.

"How the fuck you know that?" Rowdy asked him. "Say told

you if you stayed here, you couldn't be on that."

"Say ain't my mama. I'm a grown ass man."

"Oh, yeah? You told Donjae you fucking his sister?" Rolla called out.

"That's fucked up." Yah pointed his finger in Rolla's face.

"You better get your finger out my face 'fore I bite that bitch off. I said I'm hungry, nigga." Rolla didn't flinch.

"Nah. That was some foul shit, yo. I ain't tell nobody I was fucking with Shatia because she asked me not to. I don't appreciate you telling her fucking business like that either, nigga. I should fuck you up."

"I already knew," I told them.

"Same." I saw a condom wrapper in the trash on top of your blunt wraps. Two and two, yo," Lik shrugged.

"She grown. I don't give a fuck about that. You start playing with her heart and shit, I'll beat your ass though," I told him.

"You can't beat me, yo," Yah said and we all laughed.

"Forreal, yo. Shatia got bad anxiety. Don't be doing that fuck shit," Keon spoke up.

"Nigga, I know. She good," Yah twisted his face.

"Back to this nigga, Santi. Where the guns at?" Lik asked.

"Nigga, you not shooting nothing. You fitna be the bait," Rowdy told him. We already worked this shit out.

"Man, fuck that. Where the guns?" Lik asked again.

"Ask Keon." Rowdy looked through the rearview mirror.

"Fuck he talking 'bout?" I asked.

"Y'all niggas talk like a bunch of bitches. I take shit and sell shit. Sometimes it's a gun. I stayed straight for a long ass time, but detailing cars wasn't enough for the shit I need to do. But since we telling shit, Rowdy and Rolla steal cars."

"You motherfucker," Rolla threw his arms up.

"How you even know that?" Rowdy asked.

"The same way you knew my shit. People talk." Keon shrugged, hitting the blunt.

"So, all you niggas some criminals? I'm the cleanest nigga in this car. I feel good." Lik popped his collar.

"Shut the fuck up," we all said simultaneously.

All of us had some side shit going on that the others didn't know. None of this would be happening if it wasn't for Say Say and these dumb ass fucking rules. Together, we had our hands in everything and could run the fucking streets. Instead, we were all pretending to be upstanding citizens. It was bullshit.

Keon

"I'm telling you niggas now; I better not get so much as a scratch on my fucking face." Qualik was whining about the plan.

Rowdy and Rolla stole one of those old ass vans with the double doors from a junk yard. We didn't have to worry about it being seen on Santi's block because the streetlights were never fixed. If you called the police in that area, they rarely came. It always took multiple calls.

The plan was to let Lik out a few blocks away. We'd follow him with the GPS, and he would be on the phone through his AirPod so we could hear everything. We only needed to hear Santi say one word before we rolled up on them. Didn't make sense to take out his crew and leave him. He would just get another crew. We needed the head.

"You ever been shot before?" Yah asked him. "I'll take the scratch."

"This some bullshit," Lik huffed.

"You good. I would never send you to your death. I know how Santi moves. He don't want you. He knows you not in that life forreal, forreal. It's a waste of a body to him. He wants the niggas doing something in the streets. Santi wants to eliminate the competition. You good."

"I better be, or I'm telling mommy, nigga." Everybody laughed at Lik.

When we got four blocks away, we dropped Lik off in an alley, and Jae kept his eyes on the GPS. Lik was still right in front of us, and Jae's eyes didn't budge from the phone screen. I don't even think the nigga blinked.

I don't know what everyone else was feeling, but I was good. I never had to pull a trigger on a nigga, but I wasn't nervous or anxious. If these niggas were with me, I knew I was good. We all had the same goal—to get home. Money on my head, with my first child on the way ain't mean shit to me except Santi had to go.

"Just turned on the block. It's only two niggas guarding the building." We heard Lik through Donjae's speaker phone.

The GPS was interrupted from Say Say calling.

"Man, fuck this." Rowdy sped down the street of Santi's block. He parked the van in the middle of the street in front of the building. Donjae and Yah slid the doors open.

The two niggas out front pulled their guns, and Rolla shot the one closest to Lik while Yah shot the other one. Donjae and I jumped out of our side, guns in hand.

"Five minutes!" Rowdy yelled, looking back at us.

Yah shot two of Santi's niggas as they were running out of the building. They fell down the steps.

"Oh shit." Lik put his hands to his head.

"Get in the driver's seat." I pulled a gun from my side and tossed it in his hands.

"Nigga!" Lik's eyes went wide, and I laughed.

My adrenaline was going. We never discussed running into the building. Most of this shit was supposed to be done from the van. Say's brothers were more experienced, so I was following their lead. I knew the four of them were all moving to protect me and Lik. I probably could've stayed in the car with Lik, but I wanted to do my part.

Rolla announced our presence to the entire building. He stood at the front door while the rest of us moved up the steps to Santi's apartment.

"Special Delivery from Santa! If you want to make it to see your babies opening their Christmas presents, stay in your shit! We won't be here long. Santi won't know you betrayed him because he's already a dead man. Merry Christmas!"

A door cracked open, and Rowdy shot passed Jae's body. The door immediately shut after a smoke bomb came flying out of the door. Yah and Rowdy ran ahead of Jae. Rowdy kicked the door open, spraying into the apartment. Yah threw the bomb in before shutting the door. These niggas were on some military shit. I felt like I was in a game of Call of Duty.

Qualik

My heart felt like it was about to burst out of my chest. I was gripping the gun so hard, my fingers started sliding. The block was dead quiet, other than the shots coming out of the building. I could see Rolla guarding the bottom floor, eating a Snicker. All them niggas were too calm for me. I was looking and listening for police and some of Santi's niggas coming from another block.

I saw movement coming around the corner. Two niggas creeping by the side of the building. They probably thought the van was empty because it was off, and I left the side doors open so they could easily jump back in. I didn't even know how to shoot a fucking gun, but I was about to learn. I slid out of the driver's seat, managing to keep my eye on them. I ducked, creeping around to the front of the van.

They were closer to the front doors than I liked. I took a shot with my eyes closed before ducking again. Even if I didn't land a hit, Rolla would hear the shot and turn around. I peeked back up and saw him coming out the building as a shot rang out in my direction. I got on the ground and leaned against the wheel of the van. This shit had my chest hurting. I heard three more shots and knew Rolla was shooting.

I peeked up to see Rolla take a shot to the arm. "Rolla!" I called his name. My fear turned to adrenaline, and I rushed towards them, taking shots even after the last nigga standing had fallen. I knew I hit him but fuck that.

"The nigga is dead. Stop shooting." Rolla shook his head at me.

"I was trying to help you. They almost took your ass out."

"Go get in the van, nigga." Rolla went back inside the building, and I walked back to the car.

I caught my first body and couldn't even get excited about it because all my brothers were still in the building. I could calm down when we were all back in the van and headed home.

Donjae

Rowdy kicked the door of Santi's apartment open, and the second the door swung open, Yah shot. His wife stood there, holding their baby. I would've let her live, sticking to the no women no kids, but Tasaya's brothers believed in no witnesses. Rowdy shot the woman in her head. Yah rushed to grab the baby before she fell. He moved the baby to the bassinet as we moved through the apartment.

Santi peeked his head up from the kitchen island. A bullet moved past me and hit the TV.

"It's over, Santi. Ain't no making it out of here," I told him, and we surrounded the island. When I made it around to his side, my gun was on his head.

"Give me that; you don't need it," Yah snatched Santi's gun from him.

"Fuck you, Donjae! I was good to you!"

"You were," I nodded my head, but family is family."

Yah sucked his teeth and pulled a knife from his pocket. In one smooth motion, he sliced Santi's neck. Nigga stole my kill.

"What the fuck, yo?" I tapped his arm.

"Too much talking. We gotta get the fuck out of here. This ain't the fucking movies," Yah shook his head. He cut at Santi's neck until the rest of his head fell off.

"I'm going to the van." Keon made his way out of the apartment, stopping to grab an AR-15 that sat on the couch near the wife's body.

I was too stunned to leave. I never saw no shit like this close up. Yah held Santi's head in the air.

"Let's go," Rowdy tapped his chest.

We rushed out of the apartment, and Yah carried the head by its hair through the hallways and down the steps. When we made it down the steps, I could see Rolla getting into the van. We walked out the front doors, and Yah shot the no parking sign from the pole.

"Fuck is you doing, nigga?" Rowdy shook his head.

"Ms. Letty said she wanted his head on a pole," he shrugged and slammed Santi's head atop the pole.

"That shit beautiful."

I was cool with Yah fucking with Shatia until I saw how off that nigga was. It was hard to see how she could handle his wildness or how he could soften up to cater to her softness. I was going to stay out of it until my sister came to me with some shit, though.

We got into the van and Lik pulled off. We rode silently, everybody tired from the hard work we'd put in. Me, Lik, and Keon got dropped off to my car while the three of Say's brothers went to drop the van back off to the junkyard. I dropped Keon to the car shop before taking Lik home. I ended up staying at Mama's. I ain't wanna go home if Say wasn't there.

Christmas Eve

Keon

When they dropped me at the shop, I could see Beige's car parked a little way down the block. She was sitting with the lights off. I told the bitch three days, but I ain't tell her to wait on me like a stalker. I couldn't wait to get this bitch off my hands. I should've never even entertained her ass.

"I see you got my gun." She walked into the garage.

"But do you have my money?" I asked her.

"I do." She pulled the cash from her bra and counted it in front of me.

When she passed the money to me, I pulled my money counter from the shelf and counted it again.

"I might be shady in some area of life, but business is business. I wouldn't short you when I might need you again."

"You can't need me again." I passed her the gun, pulled the money from the counter, and put it in my pocket. "This it. One stop shop. I don't do repeated business. Especially not for you."

"Why not me?"

"You do too much. I'm willing to bet money that whatever you 'bout to do with that, is going to make it back to my ears. I don't like that so, this is it."

"I'm not even going to lie; it probably will. But thanks for coming through this time," she smiled, switching out of the garage.

I jumped into one of the cars I'd fixed weeks ago. The owner was still trying to come up with the money. I was going to take it back to her as a Christmas gift, but that would be after I got rid of these guns. I would fuck with the odometer and change the mileage on the car after my five-hour drive to the location and back.

I had to stop and see Rahleigh before I took that trip. She was probably already waiting on me with Lik being home and me not coming back with him. I sent her a text to come outside when I pulled up. When she opened the door of Ma Neek's house, I met her on the porch.

"Hey." She gave me a hug.

"Hey." I squeezed her tightly.

"Why you keep a whole baby from me, Leigh?"

"I don't know. At first, it was just never the right time. Then, I started weighing my options. Then it turned into me being spiteful, wondering when you would notice the changes happening to my body. Keon, I know that for the most part, you've been the man of your house for most of your life. This added responsibility is nothing for you. I love that you just take life as it comes and roll with the punches, but that's not what I want for myself. Well, that's how I was feeling. I think it's the pregnancy hormones, too. My emotions are all over the place. What I'm trying to say is, I was wrong and selfish. I want to spend the rest of my life with you. Just you. Your mother comes with that the same way my family comes with committing to me. This is the second time, that I know of, that you have risked your everything for my family and Jeru ain't even blood family. So, I'm riding with you. Forever. Wherever. Until we crash out."

"It sounds good, but I can't trust you, Leigh. You gon' have to work to earn that back. I'll figure the shit out with my mother. You don't gotta worry about that. I noticed the changes. I didn't say shit because I didn't want you to feel any less attractive than you always been. But you took something from me that I can never get back. That shit hurt."

"Keon," she sucked her teeth, "I'm ready to come home."

"I'm ready for you to be home. But I have to go handle something, and it's not safe for you to be with me. I'll be back in the morning. I promise. If you want to go home, get one of them to drop you off, but I think you should stay here since we could be having a baby any day now."

"Ok. I'll stay here until you get back."

"I'll be right back." I moved her braids from her face. "I love you."

"I love you, too."

I loved Leigh with everything in me but every time she lied to me; I was reminded that she didn't love me the way I loved her. That wasn't something that was ever going to change because we had two different love languages. I knew in my heart, it wouldn't work out with us, but I was going to thug it until we crashed out.

Shatia

Yah walked into the house at about 2 AM. I'd been sitting on the couch, watching romance comedies, waiting for him to get in. I wasn't going to be able to sleep until I knew he was ok. No one told me anything, but when I went to Ma's, no one was talking. Everyone kept peeking at their watches. That's what let me know something was going on.

"What's up?"

I rushed up from the sofa and hugged him. Yah grabbed me around my waist and kissed my cheek.

"Are you okay?" I held his face.

"Yeah, I'm good. Just tired." He moved past me and undressed.

He told me all about their night while he took a shower. I sat on the toilet seat, listening. I loved how he included me. My brothers shared stuff with their girls and even Ma, but nobody told me anything that they thought would mess with my anxiety. Yah told me everything and if he saw it was making me uncomfortable, he'd relax me. I loved how real he kept it with me. He didn't see me as fragile as everyone else did. Yah Yah helped me get my power back. How could I not love him too?

"I'm glad you made it home," I said, following him from the bathroom to the bedroom.

"Is this home?" he asked, drying behind his ears.

"I thought it was." I looked away from him. "But when you say it like that..." I climbed into bed.

"Ain't no need for you to go and get uncomfortable. We're just talking."

"Talking about what though? What are you trying to say?"

"You keep calling this home, but all my shit somewhere else. You want this to be home, only because it sounds good. You don't want this twenty-four seven. Because if you did, Israel would be out the picture." He got into bed next to me. He snuggled his head onto my breasts. Whenever he did that, I knew he'd had a long day.

"Israel is never going to be out of the picture. He's family. His family is my family, and my family is his. That's why I can't just say yes to being together. You understand so much about me but not that. So, I know it's more of your feelings about it than anything else. You're never going to be okay with our relationship."

"So, I guess we leave shit where it is. But this ain't home. Home is where the heart is, and mine can't be here because yours is somewhere else."

"Israel and I are just—"

"Friends. I know. Us, too. I guess we just gone share, and that's that on that."

Yah Yah didn't say anything else. He went to sleep while I was stuck up with racing thoughts. Once again, he let me off the hook. I didn't know if I wanted either of them to apply pressure, or if I just liked hearing them spill their feelings for me. I played in his cruddy while he slept until gunshots went off in the parking lot. Yah jumped straight up like he was never sleeping. He grabbed his gun from his pants and left out of the door. I went over to the window and peeked out. It was a woman spraying Yah Yah's car the fuck up.

She started yelling, and I cracked the window to hear what she was going on about.

"How the fuck you move to another state while I'm sitting behind bars? You got me fucked up, Yah Yah." My mouth flew open, and I opened the window more so I could see and hear.

"Beige. What the fuck you doing to my shit?" He shot near her foot.

"Oh my God," I whispered aloud to myself.

"Shoot at me again and I will send you home to your mother in a casket! How could you do that to me?"

"Do what to you? You forget how you got there? You was fucking another nigga. You took a charge over another nigga. Get your batshit ass the fuck out of here. This ain't home, Beige. Police prolly already on their way. Get the fuck out of here!" He pointed to the street.

"Fine. But you gon' fucking talk to me, nigga, and I'm not fucking playing with you." She stormed over to her car, and Yah and I both watched her pull away.

I shut the window and rushed over to the bed. I wanted to see if he would tell me what it was about without me having to ask. Before he made it upstairs, my phone rang.

"Hello?" I answered for my mother.

"The baby is coming. Meet us at the hospital."

"Ok. I'm on my way." I hung up and jumped back out the bed.

Yah walked into the bedroom. "Where you going? I know you ain't tripping off that shit out there." He pointed to the window. "That shit ain't 'bout nothing. Just my crazy ass ex-girlfriend."

"Rahleigh is having the baby." I put my tennis on.

"Fuck." Yah ran his hands down his face. "I'm never going to get no sleep.

"You don't have to go," I assured him.

"I want to. That's family. I'm fitna be an uncle again," Yah smiled.

I couldn't help but laugh at his excitement for my sister. I wish I could commit to him the way he wanted me to but for now, not having to do big life shit alone, was enough for me.

Rahleigh

"This shit hurts!" I yelled in the passenger seat of Donjae's car.

Jae kept telling me to calm down, as if I didn't have a whole ass baby making its way out of my vagina.

"Please, stop yelling." Tynee grabbed her ears.

"You can shut the fuck up because you could've ridden with Mommy and Cease." I was gripping the door handle for dear life.

"Stop talking to her like that." Jae twisted his face up at me.

"Just drive!" I yelled at him.

"You know hiding a whole fucking baby was dumb as fuck. Anything could've happened, Leigh. You went through your whole pregnancy alone when you didn't have to. Now, we're all trying to show up for you and you being a bitch. Tynee rode with us because she wanted to ride with her sister. I drove you because I wanted to be there for my sister. I don't give a fuck how bad it hurts. Fix your fucking attitude."

I started crying. I did go through my entire pregnancy alone. And even with my siblings in the car for me or my mother and Cease getting everything I needed for my hospital bag, I still felt alone. I guessed I did that to myself, but that's how I felt. Keon wasn't even here, and he wasn't answering the phone either. Everyone tried to call him, and he didn't answer anyone's call. If he was fucking some bitch, I was going to kill him.

Jae pulled up at the emergency entrance of the hospital, and Tynee and Jae rushed out of the car. Jae opened my door, and

Tynee reached for my hand. I didn't budge.

"What the fuck is you doing, Leigh?" Jae ran his hands down his face. "Come the fuck on."

"I'm not getting out of this car until I hear from Keon."

"You think that's going to keep the baby in there? Get ya dumb ass out of the car."

"No! I'm not having this baby without him.

"Oh my God." Tynee sucked her teeth and walked into the hospital.

"I'm going to keep it real with you, Leigh. Keon might not even make it to the hospital. He taking care of some shit, and the drive is crazy. But I got you. Lik got you. Sha got you. I'll stay with you, and you can squeeze my hand as hard as you want. But you gotta get out of the car, shorty."

I nodded my head, wiping the tears from my eyes. Tynee was walking out with a nurse who had a wheelchair for me. Jae helped me into the chair while Tynee pushed it, following behind the nurse.

"I'm sorry for cursing at you, Tynee. I'm just in a lot of pain."

"It's ok, Rahleigh. We got you."

I couldn't help but laugh. She heard us saying that to each other so much, she started saying it too. She was so young; she didn't even know what that meant. I hoped I never had to give her that speech for half the shit we all went through together.

Within thirty minutes, my room was full of people who weren't even supposed to be in the room. Even Uncle Damon and Say's brothers showed. I wished she was here with me. When the nurse found everyone in my room, she put them all out. She told me that I could only have one person in the room at a time. I chose Shatia. I complained to her about Keon not being there with me and not answering his phones all the while screaming through my contractions. I was about to put her ass out of the room and trade her for one of the men out there. They would let me squeeze their hand.

She was telling me all her man problems and got frustrated with me because I didn't see the problem. She had two men in love with her and not forcing her to choose. Shit. I told her to sit on the throne and let them worship her. I ain't say it to her, but that Beige bitch might give all of us a run for our money. A bitch who went crazy over a man was a different type of woman.

Shatia looked down at her ringing phone and showed me the screen. Keon was calling. Shatia put her hands up to shush me.

"Hello?" she answered the phone on speaker.

"Hey, Sha, I'm trying to reach Leigh. They said you was the only one in the room with her. Can you pass her the phone real quick?"

"She already had the baby."

"Fuck! I fucked up. She sleeping now? Tell her I'm sorry and I'm going to make it up to her. I swear—"

"Just joking. Hold on." She took the phone off speaker and put it on mute before passing it to me.

"I told you he wants to be here." She got up and left the room.

I took the phone off mute.

"Hello?"

"I'm sorry, Rocky, but I'm on my way. I just need you to keep her, or him, in there until I get there."

"And how am I supposed to do that?" I laughed.

"Ion know. Squeeze your legs together or something." We both laughed.

"I'll try. I don't know if it's a girl or boy either. So, it's a surprise to us both. Mommy and Cease are out buying clothes for both until we find out."

Keon and I stayed on the phone. We tossed baby names

out and couldn't agree on anything. He talked me through every contraction I had. I wished he was there with me. I hoped he made it here in time. I know I kept the pregnancy from him in the beginning, but I didn't want to do anymore of this on my own.

Christmas Day

Tasaya

When my plane landed, I called Rowdy to pick me up. I grabbed some breakfast while I waited. I was able to finish my food before he texted me that he was outside. I gathered my things and made my way to his truck. I couldn't help but smile like a big ass kid when I saw one of my brothers. So, when I got in the truck and saw Jae, I wiped the smile from my face.

"That's how it is?"

"That's how you left it," I told him, putting on my seatbelt.

"So, I fucked up. But not how you think. You think I fucked up because I should've left the streets alone. I think I fucked up by not telling you about it."

"They're both fuck ups to me, Jae."

"I disagree," he shook his head. "You should've never asked any of us to leave the streets. None of us want to disappoint you, and all of us have been lying and doing it anyway. This is who we are, Say. I try to leave this shit alone, but it keeps on calling me. It's like having an itchy trigger finger. I be fiendin' to get back to this shit."

I understood him because honestly, the shit wasn't easy for me either. I used Savion as motivation, but I wanted to be in the streets right along with them. It was the money for them, but it was the power for me. I liked feeling untouchable. I liked the respect that came automatically. I liked setting motherfuckers straight when they disrespected, but I didn't want any of that shit for Savion or the baby I was carrying.

"And I don't want to do it, so now what? Where do we go from here? I don't want to raise my kids in a broken home. I came up in that. Me and my brothers turned out well, but we got some shit with us. You and your siblings, too. I want to break the cycle."

"They don't have to grow up in a broken home. You ain't gotta worry about me lying to you like that again because I'm telling you straight up. I want the streets. We killed Santi."

My mouth fell open at his confession. "Jae," I sighed.

"Had to because he killed Jeru. We had to make that shit right."

I saw that Jeru died on social media. That was the only thing that made me regret not coming home when Jae did. I should've been with them

"I get it."

"But his whole shit is up for grabs and with the shit we all been doing behind your back, we can take it. I want it, Say. I'm being up front with you. I should've told you the first time, but I'm telling you now. I want to be King."

"Jae, I don't know," I shook my head. He was making that shit sound so good. The only fear I held in me was for our children.

"I do this shit a lot better with you by my side. Please, Say."

That was a fact. Without me, they would all fuck up. I kept their heads on straight. If we ran the streets the right way, it would only mean more protection for our children. Not less. But it only took one mistake from one person to make an empire fall. That wouldn't happen to us. There was nothing but solid motherfuckers on our team.

"Okay, Jae. I've been a princess for so long, I wouldn't mind being the first lady of the streets. If this shit gets too crazy though, we bow out gracefully, Jae. I need you to promise.

"I promise."

Jae pulled into the hospital parking lot, and I looked at him confused.

"Who the fuck is in the hospital?" I leaned forward.

"Well, Rolla got shot in the arm. He should be released soon, and Rahleigh is having her baby."

"Her baby?"

"Oh, Rahleigh's been hiding a fucking pregnancy for nine damn months." Jae shook his head. "She went into labor last night."

"Oh my God." I was out of my seatbelt and opening the door before he parked all the way. I knew Rolla was fine, but I was too excited to get to Rahleigh. She was going to be a great mother. Plus, I needed to curse her out because we kept secrets from everyone else, not each other.

When we made it into the waiting room, my soft ass started crying from all of the excitement everyone had on their faces to see me. Every single one of them gave me a hug and even after all these years, the love was still overwhelming.

"Jae, I really don't like this soft shit you got my sister on," Rowdy shook his head.

"Shut up. My hormones are all over the place because I'm pregnant."

Everyone went crazy with excitement, and the hugs went around again but this time, for me and Jae both.

"I am so happy for y'all. I was saving this for our Christmas dinner, but we might not make it home for that." Cease got down on one knee in front of Ma Neek.

The entire group of us looked at him like he was crazy.

"It's good, y'all. Cease and I are good," Lik cooled us off. "He a good dude." Lik dapped him up.

We nodded our heads and gave smiles, showing our support for his proposal. He didn't get to say another word because

Ma Neek screamed yes and jumped into his arms. We sent our congratulations when Keon came running from the back.

"He's here. I have a son." Keon bit his lip, trying not to cry. "Malik Jenkins."

I felt even better about our decision to take over the streets. We could never lose with the way we loved each other, and that would be the difference. The niggas in this game were heartbroken, ruthless, trying to survive. We already had everything in the world, and we just wanted more. Who was going to fuck with us?

THE END

WANT TO INTERACT WITH T'ANN MARIE & HER TEAM? JOIN OUR READERS GROUPS ON FACEBOOK!

T'ANN MARIE PRESENTS: GRANDMA'S HOUSE | Facebook

T'ANN MARIE PRESENTS: GRANDMA'S HOUSE 2.0 | Facebook

WIN PRIZES, BE APART OF LIVE BOOK DISCUSSIONS & MORE!

Join Our Mailing List:

http://eepurl.com/gU81k5

www.ingramcontent.com/pod-product-compliance
Lightning Source LLC
LaVergne TN
LVHW010605160826
845677LV00013B/3261
* 9 7 9 8 3 7 2 2 8 6 4 0 5 *